Look what p
these t

Kimberly Raye

"Highly sensual, well-developed
and sympathetic characters, plus vampire
cowboys, make this a first-rate read."
—*RT Book Reviews* on *Cody*

"A laugh-out-loud, sexy, heartwarming story
and a wonderful heroine."
—*RT Book Reviews* on *Drop Dead Gorgeous*

"Kimberly Raye's *A Body to Die For* is fun
and sexy, filled with sensual details, secrets
and heartwarming characters—as well as
humor in the most unexpected places."
—*A Romance Review*

Samantha Hunter

"Nonstop action and sexy characters…
add up to a thoroughly fun read."
—*RT Book Reviews* on *Caught in the Act*

"Samantha Hunter's magical pen
has given us a delightful book."
—*Cataromance* on *Hard to Resist*

"A steamy, romantic page-turner."
—*Coffee Time Romance* on *Untouched*

ABOUT THE AUTHORS

Bestselling author **Kimberly Raye** started her first novel in high school and has been writing ever since. Not only does she pen steamy contemporary novels for Blaze, but she's also writing a romantic vampire mystery series for Ballantine Books. Kim lives deep in the heart of Texas Hill Country with her own cowboy, Curt, and their young children. She's an avid reader who loves Diet Dr. Pepper, chocolate, Toby Keith, chocolate, alpha males (especially vampires) and chocolate. Kim loves to hear from readers. You can visit her online at www.kimberlyraye.com.

Samantha Hunter lives in Syracuse, New York, with her husband and pets. Her writing career began at age six, when she crossed out the author line on her LIFE Encyclopedia and wrote in her own name instead. Since then, she's earned a Masters in English and taught college writing for several years, as well as putting her name on seventeen Blaze novels of her own. She was a RITA® Award "Suspense/Adventure" finalist in 2008 for her Blaze novel *Untouched.* Sam is an avid reader, prefers television to movies and loves to travel. She also likes chatting online, and you can usually find her on eHarlequin.com, Twitter and Facebook.

Kimberly Raye
Samantha Hunter

BLAZING BEDTIME STORIES, VOLUME IV

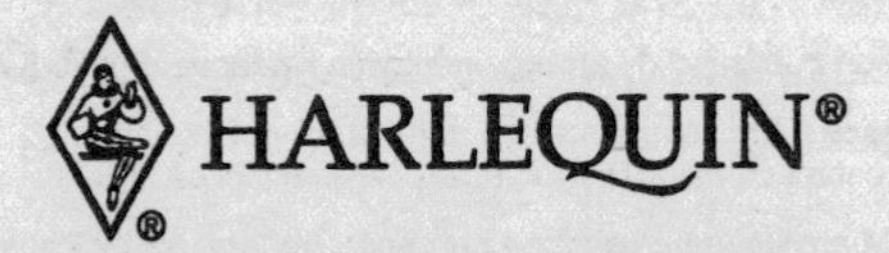

TORONTO • NEW YORK • LONDON
AMSTERDAM • PARIS • SYDNEY • HAMBURG
STOCKHOLM • ATHENS • TOKYO • MILAN • MADRID
PRAGUE • WARSAW • BUDAPEST • AUCKLAND

ISBN-13: 978-0-373-79529-1

This edition published by arrangement with Harlequin Books S.A.

For questions and comments about the quality of this book please contact us at *Customer_eCare@Harlequin.ca.*

www.eHarlequin.com

Printed in U.S.A.

CONTENTS

This story is dedicated to Debbie Villanueva
for always being such a great friend and an even
better person. I'm so thankful to have you in my life.

Girl, you totally rock, and you do it
in awesome shoes!

CUPID'S BITE
Kimberly Raye

1

THIS WAS THE LAST PLACE he needed to be.

The warning echoed in Rayne Montana's head as he stood in the shadows outside the Iron Horseshoe—a small bar and grill that sat on the outskirts of Skull Creek, Texas. He was only in town for a week. The fewer locals he ran into, the better.

Hell, the fewer people he came into contact with, the better.

At the same time, the Horseshoe was the only decent bar in his map dot of a hometown, and pretty much the only place on a Tuesday night that a man could find a woman.

And Rayne needed a woman in the worst possible way.

He pushed through the door, into the neon-lit interior. Anticipation hit him like a sucker punch to the gut. Hotter and more potent than anything he'd ever felt before, and he'd always been a lusty man.

It was different now.

He was different.

His body vibrated. His muscles clenched. His senses magnified, his perception heightened to a new level that had nothing to do with fourteen years of special ops training as part of an elite Navy SEAL unit, and everything to do with the hunger that now lived and breathed inside him.

He was clear across the room, yet his nostrils flared with the rich lilac scent of a woman sitting near the jukebox. His razor-sharp vision sliced through the cigarette haze to see a tiny spiderweb near the far corner of the tin ceiling. Taylor Swift blared from the jukebox, but the song didn't drown out the subtle slide of boots against the sawdust-covered floor.

He heard everything—the *glub-glub* as a man chugged a beer near the pool table, the sizzle of burgers popping on the grill out back, the hum of the Coors sign that flickered on the wall, the sharp intake of breath when the woman behind the bar turned and spotted him.

He stiffened and awareness skittered up his spine. He turned and found the bluest eyes in the Texas Hill Country staring back at him.

Need knifed through him. Fierce. Overwhelming. Unexpected.

Because she wasn't just one of the dozens of women he'd had in the past few weeks as he'd tried to sate the craving deep in his gut.

She was the one woman he'd wanted all of his life.

The one woman who hadn't wanted him.

She turned and took off for the back room, obviously desperate to avoid him. His chest tightened and pain twisted inside him. A crazy reaction, he knew. So what if Lucy Rivers still hated his guts?

He wasn't here for her.

She'd been his girl way back in the day and he'd been her man, but that had ended a long, long time ago. He hadn't seen her in the fourteen years since. Hell, he didn't want to see her.

Especially now.

He ignored the small voice that whispered otherwise and forced his attention back to the sharp need pushing and pulling inside him. Walking the few feet to an empty table, he grabbed a chair and sank down, his back to the wall.

He scoped out the room, his gaze going to a blonde that sat nearby. The minute his attention zeroed in on her, she felt him. She turned. Her brown eyes collided with his. Interest sparked in her gaze and her thoughts rolled through his head as clearly as if they'd been his own.

Her name was Sherry and she was a local real-estate agent. She'd just sold her first house this afternoon and she was here celebrating. She'd left the husband and the kids at home and she was now on her fourth margarita. She'd never had an affair before, but the minute her gaze locked with Rayne's she was suddenly more than willing.

She would gladly peel off her clothes. Spread her legs. Do any and everything he wanted—

He broke the connection and shifted his attention elsewhere. As starved as he was, he wasn't about to add bastard home wrecker to his ever-growing list of sins. His gaze went to the next woman.

She had red hair. Green eyes. Nice smile. Her name was different, but her reaction was the same. She wanted him.

They all did.

He shifted his attention from one female to the next. Some smiled. Some licked their lips. Others waved. One even leaned over just so, giving him a spectacular view of her bare breasts topped with rosy-red nipples.

There was no doubt. They wanted sex.

And he wanted it, too.

As fiercely as he wanted the succulent heat of their blood in his mouth, gliding down his throat, filling his body.

A vampire.

He still had trouble wrapping his mind around the concept, but there was no other explanation for what had happened to him that night two weeks ago in the Afghan mountains outside Kabul.

For what was happening to him.

Right here. Right now.

His body ached. His insides knotted and twisted. Electricity skimmed up and down his arms, making him feel more alive than ever before. Ironic considering he was stone-cold dead.

He had been. For those few brief moments before he'd swallowed the blood of his attacker, he'd been limp. Lifeless.

No more. A few ravenous sips and he'd turned into something dark. Dangerous.

A vampire who fed off blood and sex.

But not tonight.

Tonight was about drinking in the sweet, decadent energy of a woman's climax. He'd figured out early on that if he did that, he could escape the bloodlust a little longer and keep his fangs to himself.

Hopefully.

His attention shifted to the doorway where Lucy had disappeared. The urge to go after her hit him hard and fast even though he'd learned his lesson long ago where she was concerned. He'd trusted her and she'd broken his heart.

She'd dumped him without a word of explanation. Just a quick "It's over" that had cut like a dull blade straight into his heart. And damned if he'd ever understood why.

Sure, he'd wanted to ask.

To plead and beg even.

But where some kids had been raised with nice clothes and good food and a loving family, Rayne had grown up the son of an alcoholic father and a neglectful mother. He'd had nothing but his pride. And so he'd kept his distance until he'd left for West Point.

He hadn't looked back since.

But things had changed in the past few weeks.

He'd changed, and the only person likely to do any begging, should they come face-to-face, would be little Miss Lucy.

For his kiss.

His touch.

His cock.

His body stirred and he grew harder. Hungrier. In spite of it all, she had given him some of the best sex of his life. She'd been as wild as he'd been, and just as uninhibited. Together they'd been explosive.

A perfect match.

Or so he'd thought.

Memories stirred and images rolled through his head. He saw Lucy's smiling face. Felt her small hand in his. Heard the sweet sound of her laughter.

His chest tightened and bitterness welled inside him, along with something else. A deep-seated curiosity. She might have faked being happy with him, but had she faked the chemistry, too?

Maybe.

Probably.

Get over it, buddy.

Solid advice, he knew. But while she'd made it more than clear at the end that she felt zilch for him emotionally, he couldn't help but wonder if she would still react to him physically.

If she would squirm when he bit her nipple and dig her nails into his shoulders when he licked her clit and gasp when he plunged hilt deep inside her.

There was only one way to find out.

He pushed to his feet and went after her.

HE WAS HERE.

The truth snapped at Lucy's heels and followed her through the rear exit and out into the gravel parking lot behind the bar. Panic punched her in the chest as she leaned back against the building. Her palms flattened against the cool tin and she tried to calm her pounding heart.

What the hell was wrong with her?

She was Lucy Rivers. She didn't run from men. Hell, she liked men. Maybe not as often as some might think, but enough to feed the bad-girl reputation she'd inherited from her late mother and older sister.

Then again, this wasn't just any man.

This was *the* man. The one who'd made her tummy quiver and her knees quake.

Fourteen years ago, she reminded herself. No way should he have the same effect now.

Her traitorous hands trembled and she stiffened.

Okay, so her body was definitely in overdrive, but not because she was still hooked on him. It was simply the shock of seeing him out of the blue that had her heart pounding so fiercely.

He'd been so busy all these years with the military—first West Point, then special ops training, then mission after mission. He'd been too busy to come home to Texas. Not that he would have wanted to. His father had been a bastard and his mother hadn't been much better. It was no wonder Rayne hadn't bothered to show up when the old man had passed away three years ago from a heart attack.

Shortly after that, Rayne's mother had abandoned the run-down farm, packed up and moved to Arizona with some guy she'd picked up at a truck stop. With his only family gone, he'd had no ties to Skull Creek and so Lucy had given up on ever having to face him.

Shock.

That was what had her pulse racing and her hands shaking and her nipples throbbing.

"That, or maybe you're just glad to see me."

His deep, sultry voice came from out of nowhere, whispering through her head, sending her hormones into a tizzy. Lucy knew then that she could no longer avoid a confrontation. The time had come.

Rayne Montana was finally here.

And he was standing right behind her.

2

LUCY TRIED TO CALM her frantic heart as she turned to face him, but it was useless. Seeing him up close was even more of a jolt than when he'd walked in the bar.

He was taller than she remembered. His dark hair much shorter, cropped close to his head in typical military fashion. A plain white cotton T-shirt outlined his broad shoulders and heavily muscled arms. A pair of silver dog tags hung around his neck. A black slave band tattoo encircled one thick bicep and peeked from beneath the edge of his sleeve. He wore faded jeans and dusty cowboy boots and an air of danger that made her pulse race.

A day's growth of stubble shadowed his jaw and outlined his sensuous mouth. Aqua-blue eyes, as deep as the Caribbean and just as intoxicating, stared back at her and her stomach hollowed out. He looked so decadently sexy that she could have eaten him up with a spoon.

A light flickered in his brilliant gaze and if she hadn't known better, she would have sworn she'd somehow surprised him.

Ridiculous, considering he was the one who'd snuck up on her. Speaking of which, her gaze swiveled to the door. She hadn't heard it open or close. No squeak of hinges. No footsteps kicking up gravel.

She cut him a look. "How did you do that?"

His seductive mouth tilted into a grin and her heart jumped. "I'm special forces, sugar. I move quietly. I have to."

It made sense. At the same time, something didn't seem quite right. He didn't seem quite right.

His eyes glittered a little too brightly and he stared at her a little too intently.

She turned, putting her back to him as she walked a few feet away and started stacking several empty liquor boxes piled near the Dumpster. If she kept her hands busy then maybe, just maybe she wouldn't want to reach out and touch him. "What are you doing here?"

"Is that any way to greet an old boyfriend?"

"You weren't my boyfriend. You never even asked me on an official date."

"I seem to recall a lot of dates."

"Those were booty calls." She finished stacking the boxes and tossed them into the open Dumpster. "There's a difference."

They'd run with different crowds. While Rayne had been as poor as she'd been, he'd made up for it with a killer arm that had taken the Skull Creek Panthers to the state football championship two years in a row. Despite the fact that he'd lived on the wrong side of the tracks in a run-down farm off Route 62, he'd been one of the in-crowd.

Meanwhile she'd been one of those River girls. Poor. White trash. One of three illegitimate daughters of the town whore. A whore herself. Hence her nickname—Juicy Lucy.

While she'd always known who he was—they'd ridden the same school bus growing up and sat in the same class, they hadn't actually met until his senior year of high school. She'd been a sophomore back then, sweet sixteen, and he'd been just two months shy of graduation. It had been a Friday night. Football season had long since passed, but the team had been smack-dab in the middle of spring training and so Rayne had been stuck at the school until well after dark. His fix-'er-up Chevy pickup had run out of gas on the way home from practice. She'd happened by in her mom's old Bonneville and offered to give him a lift to the nearest gas station. When they'd pulled up at the Fill-R-Up, he'd told her thank you.

And then he'd kissed her.

It had been the craziest moment. One second he'd been looking at her and the next, she'd been in his arms, feeling as if she'd always belonged there. No boy—and she'd had plenty—had ever kissed her the way Rayne had.

As if he'd meant it.

They'd spent every Friday night together from then on. She would meet him down by the river after practice. Or out at his barn. Or back at her house.

Her oldest sister, Robin, had said he was using her for sex, but Lucy had known better. She'd seen the sincerity in his gaze. The genuine liking. She'd felt it whenever he'd touched her. And even more when he hadn't.

No matter what Robin believed, Lucy and Rayne hadn't spent all their time making out. They'd talked, too. About the past. The present. The future.

He'd had so many plans and she'd had so few, and so she'd done the right thing when the time had come. The day after he'd received his acceptance letter from West Point, she'd broken up with him.

He'd left shortly after graduation without so much as a

goodbye. No "let's work it out" or "let's keep in touch" or "we can still be friends." Nothing.

Proof beyond a doubt that he hadn't loved her.

"Not that there's anything wrong with a booty call," she blurted, her gaze colliding with his. It was bad enough that she'd fallen into a one-sided relationship. But to have Rayne realize exactly how she'd felt about him? No, thank you. "They're one of my specialties."

His gaze narrowed for a split second and if she hadn't known better she might have thought the idea bothered him.

But, of course, she knew better.

Her chest tightened and she pasted on her sexiest smile. "You're looking good." Her gaze narrowed just a hint in typical Juicy Lucy fashion and she licked her lips. "Good enough to eat."

Displeasure flickered in his eyes. "Careful, sugar." He stepped toward her, and instinctively she took a step back. "I might actually think you're glad to see me."

"You and every other guy inside," she said with as much nonchalance as she could muster.

He took another step and she matched him, backing up as he advanced until she came up against the building.

"That's bullshit and you know it." He stopped just shy of pressing his body against hers. "A nice, big steaming pile."

She tilted her head back and stared up at him. "What makes you so sure?"

Because I can see inside you.

That was what his gaze said, but she knew she was just imagining something more than what was really there.

Love.

That was why she'd broken up with him and let him go. Because she'd loved him. Even though she'd known that leaving was the best thing for him, she'd secretly hoped that he would stay in Skull Creek. It had been crazy. Selfish. Logically she'd known that West Point was his ticket out of a small town, away from the abuse he'd endured for so long. At the same time, she couldn't help but want him to stay. She'd loved him desperately.

But he hadn't returned the feeling.

She'd thought so at the time. She'd imagined it all—the emotional connection, the deeper intimacy, the happily-ever-after waiting on the horizon for them—just as she was imagining the strange current flowing between them right now.

"I really need to get back to work." She started to push him away, but he leaned into her, planting his arms on opposite sides of her, his palms flat against the building.

He stared at her, an intense look in his eyes, as if he'd just figured out the last piece of a puzzle. "You are glad to see me," he said as if the news surprised him.

Heat pulsed along her nerve endings and denial rushed to her lips. "I am not."

Satisfaction tugged his lips into a huge smile. "Oh, yes, you are."

"Says you."

The smile faded into pure intent. "No, darlin'." He leaned down. His lips grazed her ear and the air stalled in her lungs. "Says you. I can see it right here." His gaze caught hers and he touched her trembling bottom lip. "And here." Fingertips grazed the throbbing tip of one breast. "And here." He trailed his thumb over her crotch. Her vagina clenched in response.

Electricity zapped her. Hot. Bold. Decadent. Her skin flushed and her nerves started to tingle.

She'd never felt so turned on by a man. So desperate.

Except with him.

Only him.

"This isn't a good idea," she blurted. She ducked under his arm and started for the back door as fast as her legs could carry her.

Her days of one-night stands were over. Contrary to popular opinion, she'd been celibate for over a year. Since the day her younger sister had dropped the bomb that she was getting married.

The news hadn't come as a surprise, but it had been a wake-up call. Seeing Miranda so blissfully happy with her fiancé, rodeo star Cody Boyd, had forced Lucy to take a long, hard look at her own life, or lack of one.

At twenty-nine, Lucy had been stuck in perpetual party mode. No real relationships. No stability. No ambition. Not even a pet. Just a long list of excuses for not making something of herself—she didn't have enough money, she didn't have enough education, she didn't get any respect. The reasons had been plenty, and so had the endless string of sixty-minute men. Sex had been the one thing she'd been good at. The one thing that had fed her ego. And so she'd indulged often.

Meanwhile, her younger sister had not only crawled out from under their mother's bad-girl shadow, she'd also worked her way out of the Happy Snappy Trailer Park. She'd put herself through college, landed a good job, bought a nice house and met a great guy. Miranda had managed to do something with her life, despite the odds stacked against her.

Which meant Lucy had a shot, too.

She wanted more out of life. A college degree. A better job. A man who would stick around longer than a few hours. One who wouldn't walk away the morning after and never look back.

Rayne had already taken himself out of that category a long, long time ago, which meant no kissing, no touching, no anything.

She picked up her steps and headed for the door.

SHE'D LOVED HIM.

The truth echoed in Rayne's head as he watched her walk away. A rush of joy went through him, followed by a tidal wave of anger. All these years he'd thought she didn't give a shit about him, that she'd used him, when all along she'd loved him.

His chest went tight and his gut hollowed out. The past pulled him back and, just like that, he was eighteen years old, watching her turn her back, feeling the heartbreak and the frustration because she didn't want him anymore.

Only this time was different.

This time he could stop her.

He caught up to her in the blink of an eye and slid in front of her, effectively blocking her exit.

She walked straight into him and came up short. Her head snapped back and her eyes widened. "How did you—"

"Stay," he told her, capturing her stare and refusing to let go.

She froze, her mouth open as if she wanted to say something else, but the words wouldn't come.

She wanted to think. To turn and run, but she couldn't. His mind overpowered hers, pulling her in, willing her to relax.

To give in.

To offer herself.

He had a vivid image of her spread across a blanket in the bed of his old truck, her long legs wrapped around his waist, her wet heat sucking at his cock and holding on tight.

But the memory paled in comparison to the real thing. Warmth radiated from her lush body. His nostrils flared with the sweet, decadent scent of fresh cinnamon rolls dripping with icing.

They'd always been his favorite dessert because they'd reminded him of his grandmother. She'd made them every Sunday morning when he'd been a kid. But then she'd passed away the year he'd turned five, his father had started to drink and his mother had started to run around, and his life had gone to hell in a handbasket.

He'd never mentioned Maw Maw Ruth to anyone until he'd met Lucy. She'd listened to his stories and she'd understood his pain because she'd had so few happy memories of her own.

The day he'd heard the verdict from West Point, Lucy had met him in the barn with a basket full of cinnamon goodies and a gallon of milk to celebrate. They'd eaten every one. And then he'd licked frosting off her fingers and her breasts and every place else, and they'd had a real celebration.

The memory of her and the cinnamon rolls and the pure joy he'd felt at that moment had haunted him ever since.

No matter where he'd gone or what sort of hellhole he'd found himself in, she'd been there, too.

In his head.

His heart.

She'd been there outside Kabul the night he'd been turned, too.

His only distraction from the fear.

The pain.

The death.

His gut twisted and hunger gnawed at him. "Kiss me," he commanded, his voice deep and compelling.

Just like that the confusion faded from her expression and desire fired her eyes a deep, sapphire blue. Her lips parted. Her nipples pebbled, pushing against the thin cotton of her tank top. She slid her silky arms around his neck and her mouth touched his.

3

THIS WAS A REALLY BAD IDEA.

Despite the hunger, Rayne knew that. But then Lucy pressed herself flush against him. Her pelvis cradled his and her breasts flattened against his chest. And just like that what was left of his conscience faded.

He wanted her.

He needed her.

And she was more than happy to oblige.

She kissed him, her mouth eating at his, her tongue plunging and stroking. Her moment of denial had fled and in its place was full-blown, uncontrollable lust. He could feel the emotion boiling inside her and smell the ripe promise of sweet, energizing sex.

His gut twisted and the beast stirred, and he couldn't get close enough, fast enough. He took her in his arms and hauled her close, grinding his hips against hers with a desperation that made her gasp.

The sound bubbled against his lips, a soft vibration that stoked the fire that blazed inside him and upped his body temperature. He'd been so cold lately. So lonely. While he'd kept company with plenty of females over the past few weeks, this was different.

This was her.

The woman he'd loved. The woman who'd loved him.

He deepened the kiss, drinking in the taste of her, consuming her with a raw intensity that left her panting when he finally broke the connection.

She stared up at him, her lips swollen and slick, and his chest hitched. His muscles tightened and his mouth went dry. His fangs tingled.

"Touch me," he finally murmured when she simply stared up at him, waiting for the next command.

Her hands slid from around his neck, down his chest. When her fingertips fluttered over his groin, his heart jammed into his throat.

She tugged at the button with an expertise that told him she'd undressed many men in all the years they'd been apart. Jealousy sliced through him, sharp and painful. Not that he'd expected her to remain celibate. She was a young, healthy, desirable woman and there was no reason she should have denied herself. Especially when she'd felt that he'd turned his back on her.

At the same time, the notion of her with someone else—anyone else—fed that deep, dark part of him and urged him to toss her over his shoulder and take her far, far away where no other man could touch her.

The zipper hissed and his jeans sagged. He sprang hot and huge into her silky hands, and the irrational emotion faded in a wave of pure, drenching pleasure.

"More," he murmured after several heartbeats when she didn't do anything other than hold him and drive him mindless with anticipation.

Dutifully her fingertips played up the underside of his

erection and back down. She furrowed a path through the crisp, dark hair that curled around the base of his shaft before tracing a vein back to the ripe purple head. She cupped him again, massaging and teasing.

A drop of pearly white liquid seeped from the tip of his penis and dropped onto the inside of her wrist. Her lips parted at the sensation and his attention shifted back to her mouth. She had the fullest lips. So slick and luscious and—

"Taste me," he commanded.

Her tongue darted out and she licked her lips before dropping to her knees to carry out the command. Her soft, silky hair brushed the tops of his thighs and her warm cheek caressed his scrotum. Warm wetness closed around him and drew him in, and the world seemed to stop.

All sound faded except the frantic beat of her heart which echoed in his ears as loudly as if it were his own. For a few precious moments, he actually forgot that he couldn't feel his own heart beat any longer. That the man he'd once been was long gone and in its place was something he still couldn't comprehend. Something that scared the crap out of him.

The steady *thump, thump, thump* grew louder. More frenzied. The taste of her excitement lingered on his tongue. His nostrils flared with the ripe scent of hot passion and raw sex and sweet, luscious cinnamon.

He feasted on the picture she made, her red lips fastened around him, her eyes closed, her long, silky blond hair framing her heart-shaped face.

The feel of her, hot and greedy as she sucked at him, stirred the beast until he felt his own insides tighten and twist. His hands tingled and he clasped her shoulders.

The sexual energy sizzled into his fingertips and up his arms, funneling into the greedy whirlwind that whipped inside him, feeding it. Warmth rushed through him and he relished the sensation.

But it wasn't enough.

He needed to be inside her. To feel her explode around him. Then he would stop feeling so cold. So alone. So friggin' hungry.

She could take away the pain and make him forget.

If she wanted to.

She didn't.

The truth wiggled past the lust beating at his brain and snatched him back to reality. To the fact that she was on her knees, ready and willing to carry out every command. But only because she had no choice. No free will.

So? a voice whispered. *Take her anyway.*

But he couldn't. No matter what a monster he'd become, he wasn't that greedy or heartless.

Not yet.

He ignored the truth that whispered in his ear and hauled her to her feet. He wanted her the way she'd been in the past. Wild and uncontrollable in his arms. A slave to her own passion rather than his.

Kissing her, he indulged for one fast, furious moment before he forced himself away.

One fang grazed the fullness of her bottom lip. A drop of blood beaded and slid from the corner of the prick point. He caught the sweet heat and touched it to his tongue. Ecstasy rushed through him, followed by a gripping need that made his entire body shake violently.

He stared deep into her eyes and forced his will on her.

He could make her forget the past few minutes while he pressed his will on her. Thankfully. "You won't remember this," he managed, his teeth clenched. "Just the talking." Every muscle in his body stretched to the breaking point as he moved aside to let her open the door to the bar. "Go. Now."

She quickly obeyed.

The hinges creaked, the door slammed shut and she disappeared inside.

Thankfully.

A shudder ripped through him and his hands trembled. His vision shifted, the colors swirling until he stared through a vivid crimson haze. The urge to rush back inside, pin her up against the wall and take what he so desperately needed gripped him for a long, painful moment before he managed to turn and put one foot in front of the other.

And then he did what he should have done the moment he saw Lucy Rivers for the first time in fourteen years—he climbed into his pickup, gunned the engine and hauled ass in the opposite direction.

WHAT THE HELL HAD just happened?

The question echoed in Lucy's head as she walked in the ladies' restroom and tried to shake the crazy feeling that she'd just done the unthinkable.

She'd talked to him.

That was it.

Sure, he'd proceeded to get a little too close with his inappropriate touching, but she'd put an end to it by walking back inside.

She hadn't touched him. Or kissed him. Or did half the things she'd wanted to do.

She'd walked away from him.

So why did it feel as if she'd done so much more?

Her lips tingled. Her cheeks felt hot. A rich, potent taste that was a far cry from the iced tea she'd had earlier lingered on her tongue.

Her attention went to her reflection. She noted her pink cheeks and the faint smudge of lipstick near the corner of her mouth.

At least she thought it was lipstick.

She leaned in and touched the dark red splotch. A quick swipe and she stared at the stain on her finger. Wait a second. Was that blood?

Her gaze shifted back to the mirror and fixated on the small nick on her bottom lip. A strange image hit her and she saw Rayne reach out, his fingertip brushing her mouth before touching his own lips. His eyes fired a brilliant purple and he sighed in ectasy—

Crazy.

She'd bitten her lip in her haste to get away from him. That was it. Even more, he had blue eyes. Not purple. Blue.

Her hands trembled as she flipped on the faucet. The cold water rushed over her fingers and she splashed the refreshing liquid onto her face.

Nothing had happened between them, she told herself. And nothing would happen between them because she was now on the wagon when it came to temporary men.

Even one who made her tummy quiver.

She grasped at the thought and reached for a paper towel. She was just drying her face when the door swung inward and Becky Bartlett walked in.

"There you are," declared the waitress.

The petite brunette wore the usual Horseshoe attire—white tank and white shorts, a red bandana tied around her neck and an exasperated expression on her face.

"I've been looking everywhere for you," Becky rushed on. "Jake Culpepper and his buddies want cosmos and I can't make anything more complicated than a Jack and Coke. You have to get your butt behind the bar right now."

"Cosmos?" Lucy tossed the paper towel and followed Becky out. "Are you serious?"

"They've given up beer completely." She rounded the corner and pushed through the doorway leading behind the bar. "That was the deal if they wanted to get out of the house. Their wives want them to be more understanding. According to some stupid seminar the wives are taking, that means role-playing. The men are stuck drinking cosmos and appletinis while the wives guzzle Bud Lite during Bunko."

"That's ridiculous."

Becky shrugged and reached for the martini glasses. "That's the SCANCs."

The SCANCs, short for Skull Creek Association of Newlywed Couples, were a group of brand-new wives eager to make their marriages successful. They attended weekly seminars on how to argue more effectively and how to get their men to mow the grass on command.

The husbands, desperate to appease their new brides, went along with most of the rules, whether it meant sucking down froufrou cocktails on poker night or eating salads instead of chili cheese fries. Zeke, the owner of the Horseshoe, had even added a light menu to the bar's staple of burgers and chicken fried steak sandwiches to appeal to all the SCANC husbands. Now the bar served up everything from fresh fruit plates to vegetables with yogurt dip.

Even though Lucy had never walked down the aisle, she'd gotten an up-close and personal look at the SCANCs by spending every morning of the past six months with the late Mrs. Arthur J. Moon.

Lucy had taken the second job to help earn enough money to put a down payment on a house. She'd run errands and taken Miss M to bingo three times a week and done any and everything that the old woman had asked of her.

Mrs. M had passed away a few weeks ago from a massive heart attack. She'd been seventy-eight and widowed, with eight marriages to her credit. While most of the SCANCs wanted longevity when it came to wedded bliss, they'd looked to Mrs. M with an extreme amount of awe. Hey, it was hard enough to snag one man good enough to marry, much less eight.

Miss M, even though she'd cheated on husbands one through seven (a definite no-no among the SCANCs), had been considered an expert when it came to matrimony (and after eight weddings, she had all the really good connections when it came to cakes and flowers). Not only had she been allowed to maintain her SCANC membership, she'd served as president for three consecutive terms.

She'd also been the owner of an obnoxious teacup poodle named Cupid.

Lucy, of course, hadn't known the dog was obnoxious when she'd brought him home after the reading of the will. Rather, she'd thought he was a cute ball of fluff and that Miss M—despite her snobby ways and impossible-to-please attitude—had actually liked her. Why else would she hand over the ticket to relationship nirvana?

Rumor had it that Cupid's canines were as good as arrows and that he'd snagged every one of Miss M's eight husbands. She'd brought home the prospective suitors and, bam, Cupid had sunk his teeth into them. They'd each fallen madly in love with Miss M, which explained why every SCANC in town was hot to take the dog off Lucy's hands.

They all believed the hype and wanted some added assurance for their new marriages.

Lucy, herself, wasn't one-hundred-percent certain she believed the hearsay, but she'd brought Cupid home with her anyway on the off chance that Cupid was the real deal (and not just one of Satan's minions).

"Mrs. Wilhelm hasn't called, has she?" Lucy poured cranberry juice into a shaker while Becky arranged the glasses on a tray.

"Not that I know of. Why?"

"She's trying to get me to pay for a custom-made quilt she bought at last year's county fair. Cupid jumped the fence yesterday and shredded it."

"I told you. Just say the word and I will gladly take him off your hands. I could certainly use him tonight," Becky added as she reached behind her and untied her apron. "I need you to stay late and cover for me. I have to duck out early."

"But I'm tending bar. I can't cover tables, too."

"Please, please, please." She stashed the apron under the counter. "Jimmy—that's his name—works offshore and this is his last night home. If I don't meet him now, it'll be two weeks before we can get together again. I don't have a cute little dog to help snag the man of my dreams. I have to do it myself, which means I can't give Jimmy a chance to forget all about me."

"Absence makes the heart grow fonder."

"Out of sight, out of mind," Becky countered. "Come on, Lucy. I really think he might be the one."

"That's what you said about Luke last week and Bill the week before that."

She shrugged. "So I don't have the greatest track record. At least I'm persistent. If I keep hanging in there, I'm bound to hit the jackpot. And this could be it. Tonight's the night. I can feel it. Please." Her pleading gaze whittled away at Lucy's resolve.

"Go on. Get out of here before I change my mind."

"You wouldn't do that." The waitress grinned. "Beneath that big, bad reputation of yours lurks the heart of a true romantic."

"You wish," Lucy said, but she couldn't resist the smile that tugged at her lips. Becky was right. She'd finally traded her cynicism for hope—pain-in-the-ass Cupid proved it—and now she couldn't help but understand Becky's plight. She, too, wanted to find that one special man to share the rest of her life.

She wanted someone she could talk to. Be herself with. Love.

The way she loved Rayne.

Correction, the way she'd loved Rayne. As in past tense. Once upon a time. Ages ago.

Never again.

Even if he was even sexier than she remembered.

"I owe you." Becky's voice effectively distracted her from the disturbing thought.

The waitress gave her a quick hug and grabbed her purse from behind the bar. Just as she disappeared, Zeke slammed the bell in the kitchen. "Order up."

Before Lucy could turn, a shout came from a table full of camo-clad men. "Where are our cosmos?"

"I've been waiting twenty minutes for my veggie dip," another man added. "It's bad enough I have to eat the stuff. At least I could get it before my arteries start to harden." The comments echoed around her and for once Lucy welcomed the distraction.

The last thing she wanted to think about was Rayne Montana and how sexy he was and what—if anything—had transpired in the back alley between them.

Talking, she reminded herself. End of story.

4

HE WASN'T GOING to think about her.

Not about how much he wanted her. Or how good she'd tasted. Or how he could still hear her heartbeat even after three hours.

Rayne gripped the steering wheel tighter. He'd been driving ever since he'd left the Horseshoe. Trying to clear his head. To unwind.

A useless effort.

He was too worked up. Too hungry.

The two-lane paved road he'd been following gave way to gravel. Tires kicked up dust as he hauled ass the half mile to the railroad tracks.

The Chevy pitched as he went over the ties. A half block down, he hung a left onto the one and only road that ran parallel with the tracks. He passed the Happy Snappy Trailer Park and his chest tightened.

His gaze shifted to the overgrown ditch on his right. That was where he'd run out of gas the night they'd met. It had been late and hers had been the only trailer in the park with the porch light on. He could still see her standing in the doorway in her oversize Cowboys T-shirt and a pair of sweatpants. She'd been even prettier up close and he'd understood right away why ninety-nine percent of the guys at school had a hard-on for her. But there'd been something else about her.

She'd had a pair of reading glasses perched on her nose and a needle in her hand. She'd been fixing the hem on a worn plaid kitchen curtain.

The sight had been so different from all the rumors he'd heard about her—that she spent her spare time prancing around in skimpy clothes and primping in front of the mirror and watching sex tapes—and it had turned him on even more than her lush curves hidden beneath the huge T-shirt.

He'd realized right then that there was more to Juicy Lucy Rivers than the hot sexpot image she portrayed. She'd had a softer side; she'd just refused to show it because she hadn't wanted to get hurt.

But he'd seen the real girl back then, and he'd fallen for her. Hard.

His cock throbbed and he slammed his foot down on the gas pedal. The truck lurched and ate up gravel at a frightening pace until the road finally dead-ended into an overgrown dirt driveway marked by a falling-down mailbox and a red-and-white FOR SALE sign.

He pulled in and killed the engine in front of the run-down two-room house where he'd grown up. The place sat surrounded by thirty-six acres of overgrown pasture and trees.

At one time, it had been his grandmother's spread. Clean and well-cared for. The gardens tended, the fields plowed. The house freshly painted. But then the old woman had died, his father had lost his job at the railroad and the drinking had started.

The house had deteriorated after that. The tin roof had

rusted and the white paint had peeled. Most of the red shutters had fallen off. The porch sagged and the front window had been broken, thanks to a whiskey bottle that had been meant for Rayne's head.

His father had been so mad that night.

More so than usual, because his mom had taken off for some bar with some guy and his father hadn't been able to deal with either. He'd cursed and carried on about how she was no good and then he'd shifted his rage to his son.

Bastard.

The old man's voice echoed and Rayne hesitated just shy of grabbing the door handle. There were too many bad memories and he had enough to contend with right now. His insides twisted and the hunger clawed at him.

A faint rustle drew his attention and he turned, his gaze picking out the pair of beady black eyes that stared at him from the far distance near a patch of cedar trees.

The throb of a pulse echoed in his ears and the scent of warm blood spiraled through his head. His gut tightened and his fangs tingled and a hiss worked its way up his throat.

The animal bolted and it took everything in Rayne to resist the urge to go after it and take what he wanted, needed, like the predator he now was.

He wouldn't. Not now. Not here.

He fought the demon inside him and focused on the house. He couldn't believe that anyone in their right mind would want to buy the place, but there'd been a message on his cell phone from a local real-estate office last month. He'd had an offer. A cash offer. All he had to do was show up, sign the papers and the money was his by the end of the week.

He'd been neck-deep in Afghanistan at the time and so he'd ignored the request.

But things were different now.

The money would be enough to help him get away from everyone and everything, disappear, and so he intended to take it and hit the road before the Navy showed up. He'd been missing two weeks now, which meant they would start looking for him any day.

The first week they'd undoubtedly assumed he was sleeping off a hangover somewhere. His buddies did it all the time. After a particularly nasty mission they'd go on a drinking binge, desperate to drown the memories of what they'd just seen and done. But one week was usually long enough to bury the memories down deep and get your ass back in gear. Two at most.

Three?

Something was definitely wrong.

He'd either cracked from the pressure of doing two straight special ops tours in Afghanistan, or he was dead. That was what the higher-ups would think. His Master Sergeant would immediately opt for number one. She thought he was too good to get himself killed and so she would file the proper papers and put him on the Navy's AWOL list. And then, she would come looking for him.

She commanded an elite unit that looked after their own. She wouldn't stop until she'd accounted for all of her men. Alive or dead.

Or undead in this case.

He hadn't just disappeared that night two weeks ago outside Kabul. He'd been attacked.

Killed.

He'd suffered over twenty-five knife wounds to the chest. Fatal wounds that had him bleeding out into the dust. He'd glanced up through a pain-riddled haze and seen the faces of the men he'd thought to be merely terrorists.

Biting at him.

Sucking his blood.

Consuming him.

He'd closed his eyes and thought of Lucy. Her blue eyes had pulled him in and soothed away the hurt. He'd taken one breath. Then two. Then the air had stalled and that had been the end.

Or so he'd thought.

But his attackers had taken more than just his life. They'd stolen his humanity and replaced it with something he still didn't fully understand.

The uncontrollable thirst.

For sex. And blood.

Selling the house was the only solution now. He could take the money and disappear.

That was what he was going to do.

What he had to do.

The Realtor would drop off the papers tomorrow and all he had to do was sign them and hand them back over. And then it would be done.

He headed around the back of the house toward the giant red barn that sat in the distance. It looked like the rest of the place—old and weathered—but there was something inviting about it framed against the moonlit sky.

His Maw Maw Ruth had taught him how to milk her favorite cow in that barn. She'd showed him how to pick out eggs. How to feed the chickens. She'd hugged him when he'd scratched his knee up in the hayloft and picked him up when he'd fallen off the tractor seat. She'd been the only one who'd ever loved him and the old barn reminded him of that.

He hauled open the double doors and walked into the musty interior. The scent of hay and horses tickled his nostrils, along with the faint aroma of vanilla extract. His gaze went to the yellow overalls with the pink daisies hanging near the doorway and the backs of his eyes burned.

Memories stirred, but he fought them back down. He didn't have time for this. Dawn would be coming soon.

Closing the barn door, he shoved the bar into place and locked it from the inside. A quick leap and he reached the hayloft high above the barn interior. He checked the one window to make sure it was latched before he pulled off his boots and shirt. Burying himself beneath a thick stack of hay, he let the darkness surround him.

And the warmth.

He'd slept in this very hayloft so many times. Hidden in it to escape his father. He'd even brought Lucy here. They'd sat in this very spot and talked about his plans for the future. He'd wanted to make the SEAL team and go on special missions for the government. While she hadn't really had any concrete plans, she'd loved to sew. He'd encouraged her to do something with it, but she'd been insecure. Scared.

He knew the feeling.

He knew her.

Christ, he still couldn't believe it.

She loved him.

Then and now.

Not that the truth made one bit of difference. It wasn't as if they could pick up where they'd left off. He was a vampire for Christ's sake.

Still, the knowledge that she'd felt something for him, that she still felt something, whispered through him and chased away the cold. The horror of the past two weeks faded and for the first time since he'd been bitten, Rayne Montana felt himself relax a little.

He was home now.

For a little while anyway.

And then he slept.

5

"YOU'RE HORNY," Robin Rivers declared. She stood in front of Lucy's dresser mirror and swiped her lips with Crimson Kiss. "When I don't get any for a few weeks, I go totally nuts, too." She licked her lips together and dabbed at the corners. "I'd hump a tree branch if it smelled like Tommy Hilfiger." She handed the tube to Lucy, who sat on the edge of her four-poster double bed. Lucy had picked the bed up at a yard sale a few weeks ago when she'd moved into the house. It was a far cry from the full-size mattress she'd shared with her two sisters while growing up and she couldn't help the slither of pride that went through her.

"Ye old hormones, little sis," Robin went on. "That explains everything. That and the fact that Rayne Montana is one fine hunk of man." She wiggled her eyebrows. "Any woman in her right mind would jump him."

"I'm not horny and I didn't jump him." Lucy pushed to her feet and grabbed the pile of discarded clothes Robin had just rifled through while looking for the one perfect blouse to borrow for her hot date with Jimbo Ferris.

Jimbo played the violin for a Southern rock band that had been performing at a small dive out near the interstate.

He was cute, gainfully employed—at least on the weekends—and the only single man in the county over the age of eighteen that Robin Rivers hadn't slept with.

Yet.

"At least not in reality," Lucy added. Thanks to Rayne's sudden appearance, she'd fantasized about him all night. She'd kissed him, stroked him, tasted him. "It was just a dream." She'd opened her eyes that morning to find Cupid gnawing on the rug that matched her new yellow comforter and the bed beside her as empty as when she'd first climbed in the night before. "Just a very real, very vivid dream."

"A very real, very vivid wet dream," Robin reminded her. "Which smacks of horny to me." Her older sister arched an eyebrow and reached for a tube of mascara. "When's the last time you got laid? A week? A month?"

Try a year. "Something like that."

"No wonder you can't control yourself." Robin pointed the mascara wand at her. "I know you're trying to do this whole about-face thing, but the truth of the matter is, women like us aren't cut out for celibacy. You should go out and find a man."

"I don't have time to find a man. I'm pulling double shifts to make my mortgage." And afford the new sewing machine she'd bought last week. "I don't have time for a man." She started folding the tanks and tube tops that her sister had just picked through.

Lucy had an endless collection of them, along with dozens of miniskirts and short shorts and corset tops. At one time, she'd been proud of the fact that she could slide on the skimpy clothes and actually look good in them. Now, it just didn't seem like enough to show for thirty years of life.

Which was why she was working hard to change things. Next week she would start her first design class at Travis County Community College. After that, it was just a matter of time until the rest of her life fell into place. A better job. A real relationship.

Not that she had even a slim hope of staying on track with Rayne Montana back in town. He'd been permanently planted in her brain since the moment he'd waltzed into the Horseshoe last night. She'd tried to concentrate after their encounter out back, but she'd made a mess of things. She'd served old man Farley a Peach Schnapps and iced tea rather than his usual Jack and whiskey. Meryl Winters had gotten Ed Hallsey's Bloomin' Onion, while Ed had done fierce damage to his cholesterol with Meryl's Hot-As-Hell wings. She'd spilled three beers, given the wrong change and stabbed herself with a corkscrew, all because of him.

"You know what you need?" Robin's voice pushed past the memories clogging her brain. "You need Andre."

"Who's Andre?"

"My F.B." She grinned. "My fu—"

"I know what an F.B. is," Lucy cut in. "And no thank you." She finished folding the last skimpy item of clothing and deposited it into a dresser drawer. "I've had enough one-night stands to last a lifetime. I don't need another."

"Really? Let's see, you're having wet dreams about a man you say you can't stand. Clearly you're not completely and totally sexually satisfied." Robin eyed her. "That, or you're still hooked on him."

"I am *not* hooked on him." Her lips tingled and she stiffened.

Robin was right. Not the part about Lucy still being hooked on Rayne. Not *no,* but *hell, no.* Rather, she was right when she said that Lucy needed a man.

She'd never gone an entire year without sex. Geez, she'd never even gone six months. Her longest dry spell had been three months and fourteen days. She'd been so desperate that she'd done one too many shots and hooked up with Cyrus Wallaby. He'd been the water boy for the football team. He'd also been voted Most Studious. And Most Likely to Die a Virgin.

She was pushing one year and five days now. No wonder she was acting loony. She was weak. Needy. Desperate.

It made sense that she would fantasize about Rayne. She would no doubt do it again if she didn't break her dry spell. And fast.

Lucy sat down on the corner of the bed. Cupid nipped at her ankles and she snatched her legs up underneath her. "So what's Andre like?"

"He's had all his shots."

"That's not what I meant."

"He's great in bed."

"That's not what I meant either."

"I know. You're missing the point."

"Which is?"

"It doesn't matter what he's like. That's the beauty of it. It doesn't matter what kind of car he drives or what he looks like or what he does for a living or if he likes the Dallas Cowboys or the Houston Texans. All that matters is what he wants. He wants sex. You want sex. There are no games. No questions. No expectations. Nothing but the two of you doing the nasty for an hour or so and then he's out of your life. You forget about him and he forgets about you." She grinned. "Until you want to get busy again, that is." She scribbled a phone number down and tucked it into Lucy's cleavage. "Call him."

SHE WAS *NOT* CALLING ANDRE.

Lucy made that vow as she fished the paper from between her breasts, dropped it onto the dresser and climbed into the shower. She was desperate, but not that desperate.

Yet.

The word popped into her head, haunting her as she pulled on her work outfit. She swiped her lips with a pale pink gloss before herding Cupid into the laundry room, where she'd set up his doggie bed and his food and water bowls.

"I'll be back soon," she vowed.

He started to bark, the sound sharp and piercing, and she seriously contemplated dropping him off at the local animal shelter.

But then that was what everyone wanted.

In the few weeks since Miss M had passed away, Lucy had had three visits from Eileen Warner who supervised the shelter. The woman had left each time with a frown on her face and a pinch between her eyebrows because she hadn't been able to find any excuse to remove the animal from Lucy's custody. She, like the rest of the SCANCs, was itching to get her hands on Cupid.

Lucy summoned her most optimistic smile. "How about when I get back we watch TV together? Or we can play fetch?"

Cupid answered by growling and sinking his teeth into the toe of Lucy's boot.

Lucy grimaced and shook the animal off. "I'll take that as a yes." She backed up and closed the door before the dog could launch into attack mode.

She ignored the incessant barking, snatched up her keys and tried to forget Robin's suggestion. She'd been horny before and never had she resorted to propositioning a stranger.

Okay, so maybe once or twice. But she'd been different back then.

She'd been a carbon copy of her mother and older sister, and so she'd carried on the family tradition of picking up men. Oddly enough, it hadn't really been about sex. She'd wanted to feel desirable.

Valued.

Loved.

The endless string of men had filled the void. For a few hours anyway. But once the next morning had rolled around, she'd been back to feeling empty. Worthless. Alone.

No more.

She was changing and she wasn't going to let Rayne Montana and his impromptu appearance throw her for a loop. She'd seen him, which meant the initial shock was over. No way would he have the same effect if she ran into him again.

Lucy held tight to that hope as she headed to work, poured beers and did her best to ignore the anticipation building in the pit of her stomach. A feeling that grew as the night wore on.

He was coming.

She wasn't sure how she knew. She just did. The certainty of it made her move that much faster and set her nerves on edge.

"Would you slow down? You're making the rest of us look bad." Becky came up beside Lucy and started popping the tops off four beers. "What's wrong with you? Are you coming down with something?"

"Yes." A bad case of lust. "I took a decongestant for this cold I have and it's making me a little antsy."

"Since when do you have a cold?"

She faked her best cough. "Since this morning."

"And here I thought you were acting like a nut because Rayne Montana is back in town."

"Why would I care if he's back?"

"Because you used to have the hots for him, that's why."

"FYI, he had the hots for me, not the other way around."

"So you couldn't care less that he's sitting in that corner over there, staring at you?"

She whirled and sure enough, he sat at a small table next to the jukebox. He wore faded jeans, a plain black T-shirt and the same dusty brown cowboy boots he'd had on yesterday. His dark blue gaze collided with hers and her heart jammed into her throat.

So much for the initial-shock theory.

"He ordered a Corona," Becky said, holding up the bottle, a lime wedged on the top. "He asked for you to bring it to him."

Like hell.

That was what she wanted to say, but Becky was looking at her as if she'd grown two heads. She was the infamous Lucy Rivers, after all. She made men nervous and anxious and desperate, not the other way around.

But then Rayne wasn't just any man.

He was *the* man.

The thought wedged itself into her brain before she could slam the door shut. Her pulse quickened and her heartbeat revved that much faster.

"You don't have a fever, too, do you?" Becky touched a manicured hand—tiger-striped tips with pink rhinestones—to Lucy's forehead. "You don't feel warm, but your cheeks are flushed."

"It's just a cold." Lucy licked her suddenly dry lips. "Really."

Becky didn't look convinced. "I bet you've got one of those internal fevers. My aunt Jenny Mae gets those all the time. It's where the fever's on the inside, trying to get out only it's not strong enough. She rubs on a bunch of calamine lotion and it clears right up."

"Isn't that for poison ivy?"

"Duh." She gave Lucy a what-planet-are-you-from? look. "Of course it's for poison ivy. It forms a protective coating on the skin."

"And it benefits a fever how?"

"If the fever's fighting to get out and you put on a protective barrier, then it keeps the heat contained inside. Once you've got it contained, all you have to do is load up on Tylenol which shoots the fever to hell and back." She gave Lucy another once-over. "If you're not feeling up to it, I can take the table for you."

She wanted to accept Becky's offer, but Lucy was never too busy for a customer. She'd had a root canal last year and she'd still managed to take old Caleb Jenkins a double order of nachos and a glass of iced tea. And the time she'd twisted her ankle? She'd hopped over to Jimmy Dietrich and dropped off his extra-large bowl of chili—no onions—and an ice-cold draft and a double order of chile lime chicken wings. She had an entire host of regulars that requested her and tipped big, and so she always found the time and made the effort when someone asked for her by name.

Becky knew that, and so did everyone else.

She grabbed the beer bottle, pasted on her sexiest smile and headed straight for Rayne Montana.

6

"THAT'LL BE THREE-FIFTY." Lucy set the beer in front of Rayne and tried to calm her frantic heartbeat. He smelled so good—a mix of leather and fresh air and an edge of danger—that was fiercely intoxicating. Her hands trembled.

He held out a twenty. "Keep the change."

She grabbed the bill, her fingers brushing his. Electricity zipped up her arm and firebombed between her legs.

"I..." She licked her lips and fought for her voice. "Um, thanks."

She started to turn, but his voice stopped her. "Why don't you sit down?"

She ignored the butterflies in her stomach and tried to keep the quiver from her voice. "I'm working."

"Everybody gets a break." He patted the seat. "Sit down and we'll catch up. That or you can tell me to get the hell out. But then everyone in here is liable to wonder why you're being such a bitch. If you really hated me, you wouldn't waste your time."

"I don't hate you." She wasn't sure why she said it. Better to have him think it was true. At the same time, she couldn't quite let him believe it. He'd heard it too often from his father for all those years and she'd seen how it had hurt him. She didn't want to add to that hurt.

Not that she would, of course. He would have to care about her for it to make a difference. Which he didn't.

Still…

Something softened inside her and suddenly taking a break didn't seem like such a bad idea. "Five minutes." She perched on the edge of the chair. "I'm really sorry about your dad."

He stiffened and a hard glint lit his eyes. "Don't be. He brought it on himself."

"I'm not sorry for him." She stared into his eyes. "I'm sorry for you."

The glint faded and the tension seemed to ease from his muscles. "Thanks."

"Miranda's getting married," she heard herself blurt out, eager to kill the silence that stretched between them. Not the uncomfortable kind, but the soft, warm variety that made her remember all their talks in the hayloft. "He's an ex–rodeo cowboy. Maybe you've heard of him. Cody Boyd?"

"Can't say that I have. I've been out of touch for a while. It's been one mission after the next."

"Sounds exciting."

"It used to be, but now it's just routine."

"So why do you keep doing it?"

"It's my job."

Or it used to be.

She wasn't sure why she had the sudden thought. Just that it was suddenly there in her head.

"There's a new spray tan booth at the fake-'n'-bake salon," she heard herself rush on, eager to shift them to a less personal topic. "And there's a second window open at the post office. The Panthers have been doing really good this year. We might actually make it to state—"

"Relax."

"Excuse me?"

He leaned back in his chair, his eyes fixed on hers. "You're nervous."

"I am not."

"Then you must be really scared."

"Please." She shook her head and summoned a laugh. "I'm not afraid of you."

"No, sugar." He leaned forward, his elbows on the table, his face coming close to hers. "You're afraid of you." His thigh brushed hers and heat rippled through her. "You're afraid if you sit here for too long—" he winked "—you'll be overcome with lust and you'll jump my bones."

"In your dreams, buddy."

The grin faded from his face and a hungry light gleamed in his eyes. "Exactly." His eyes gleamed brighter, almost unearthly, and goose bumps danced up and down her arms. "What about you?"

He ran a strong fingertip up the side of his bottle, gathering the drops of condensation as he went, and she could have sworn she felt the slow drag up the middle of her back. Her nipples hardened and her nerves hummed.

"What have you been dreaming about lately?" he added, his voice low and deep and stirring.

You.

She bit back the word before it could slip past her traitorous lips and shrugged. "I don't waste my time with dreams." She gave him a knowing look. "They're not near as much fun as the real thing."

Most men would have taken that as a come-on, but Rayne stiffened. His gaze narrowed and she had the distinct impression that she'd hit a raw nerve.

But then his expression eased and she knew it was just her deprived hormones making her imagine things.

He would have to care about her to be jealous and he'd already made it obvious that he didn't.

Even if he did have the strangest light in his eyes. As if she was the one thing did care about. The only thing.

"Are you done with the military?" The words poured out of her mouth as she tried to distract herself from the sudden butterflies in her stomach. "Are you on vacation? Are you on some secret military mission to scope out Mr. Bixby's new herd of cows? What?"

He opened his mouth as if he were about to tell her something, but then he shrugged. "Yeah," he finally said.

"You're on vacation?"

"I'm scoping out cows. See, the Russians are out to implant a chip in Bixby's herd so that they can take over the town." He added in a hushed whisper, "We're on the verge of a full-blown cattle invasion."

A grin tugged at her lips. "You're full of it."

"Maybe, but I got you to smile."

"You also dodged my question."

"A double whammy. Am I good or what?"

Too good. He always had been. That was why she couldn't get him out of her head. She was deprived and he represented hot, steamy, mind-blowing sex. She couldn't help but be attracted to him. It had nothing to do with the fact that she still had feelings for him.

He looked good. He smelled good. He had a penis.

End of story.

"Ruth left me the ranch when she died." His deep voice cut into her thoughts. "I didn't know it at the time. She made arrangements for my parents to keep living there, but she left specific instructions that if anything happened to them, the property was to go to me." He ran a hand over his face before his gaze collided with hers. "I'm selling it and the Realtor needs me to sign the final papers."

Which explained his sudden appearance. At the same time, she couldn't shake the feeling that he was holding back and there was more to him being here than a simple real-estate transaction.

Before she could dwell on the notion, he reached out. His fingers brushed back several strands that had come loose from her ponytail. "You always did have the softest hair."

"And you always had the smoothest pickup lines."

"If memory serves, you're the one who picked me up."

"Only because you ran out of gas. You're the one who kissed me when I dropped you off."

"You wanted me to kiss you."

Amen. She stiffened. "Is there a point to this conversation?"

"We were good together." The blue of his eyes darkened as he stared at her. "We could still be good together."

Staring into his eyes, she found herself entertaining the notion. But then she blinked and sanity zapped her.

"That's it. Break's over." She scooted back her chair and pushed to her feet. "It's been great catching up, but I really have to—" The words stumbled to a halt when she felt his hand on her arm.

"Spend the night with me." His gaze caught and held hers. "One more night. Just the two of us. For old times' sake."

Heat skittered down her spine and desire bolted through her. She wanted to. She wanted it so much that it suddenly scared her. "I—I can't." She shrugged away from him and forced herself to her feet.

"You can't or you won't?"

"Both." She swallowed, ignoring the sudden image that popped into her head—of the two of them, bodies tangled, mouths eating at each other. "I, um, already have a date." And then she turned and headed back behind the bar before she did something really stupid.

Like kiss him.

Or worse.

She ignored several beer requests and a signal from Rich Winters, who wanted ketchup for his onion strings. Instead, she reached for the phone that sat under the counter and punched in the number imprinted on her brain.

A loud ring echoed in her ear and she tried to calm the frantic beat of her heart.

Desperate times called for desperate measures. And she knew, as surely as she knew her own name, that she wouldn't be able to walk away from Rayne if he cornered her again. Not tonight. Or tomorrow.

Not in her present state.

She was too worked up. Too needy. Too horny.

That was why she'd found herself forgetting how much he'd hurt her in favor of how good it would feel to fall into bed with him just one more time.

It wasn't him, she reminded herself. It was the fact that he had a penis. Once she broke her fast she wouldn't be such a hormonal hurricane. Then she could forget the way he stroked that damn beer bottle and the way his lips closed over the mouth and the way his Adam's apple moved up and down as he chugged the gold liquid.

And she knew just how to prove it.

The phone rang once more. The shrill sound lasted a split second before she heard a clear, distinct "Yo."

She put her back to the crowd and faced the row of bottles lining the wall. "Andre?" she murmured into the receiver.

"Who's this?"

"A friend of mine gave me your name. She said you might be able to help me with a problem I'm having."

"Who's the friend?"

"Robin Rivers."

"When do you need help with this problem?"

"Tonight."

"Let's see, it's a quarter past nine right now." He went silent for five frantic heartbeats. "Meet me at the Holiday Trails Motel out on Route 16 in an hour. Room 24."

She glanced over her shoulder at Rayne, who sipped his beer, a dark look on his face as if he knew what she was up to and didn't like it one little bit.

Hardly.

He was clear across the room. The only thing he might know was that she wasn't as immune to him as she pretended to be. Her nipples were rock-hard, pressing against the thin cotton of her tank, twin beacons that testified to her arousal. Her legs quivered and her panties felt damp. Her cheeks burned and the urge to duck her head into the ice machine to her left was nearly unbearable.

Especially when he lifted his bottle in salute and blew her a quick kiss. There was no mistaking the warm sensual press of lips at the base of her spine and shock bolted through her. She whirled, but there was no one standing behind her.

Her startled gaze shifted back to Rayne, who sat clear across the room. Eyeing her.

"Make it a half hour," she blurted before sliding the receiver into its cradle.

She was imagining things. Out-of-this-world sensual things which meant she needed a man right this very second.

She whipped off her apron, tossed it under the counter and reached for her purse. She ducked into the kitchen and gave Zeke the spiel about the internal fever and her urgent need for calamine, before slipping out the back door.

And then she climbed into her car and headed for the Holiday Trails Motel.

SHE'D SET UP A SEX DATE.

Rayne wouldn't have believed it if he hadn't heard with his own ears. But then, he heard everything thanks to his heightened senses.

The beep of the numbers as she'd dialed. The frantic in and out of her breath as she'd waited anxiously for an answer. The catch in her voice as she'd asked the voice on the other end for help with her problem.

A sex date.

Sonofabitch.

Not that he had anything against a sex date as long as both parties were willing and took the proper precautions. But this was Lucy. His Lucy. He'd missed her for so long.

Fantasized about her night after night. Relived every moment with her every friggin' day since she'd broken his heart. And damned if he was going to sit by and just let another man have her.

Particularly when he was the one who'd worked her up in the first place.

The goal had been to talk her into his bed. He'd come here to do just that. To remind her of the past, of how good they'd been together, of how good they could be, and have her choose him willingly.

Because she wanted him.

She did.

He'd felt the push-pull of lust inside her, seen the raw desire gleaming in her eyes, smelled the scent of warm, ripe, willing woman, and heard the excited staccato of her heart.

And while he'd been more than willing to wait and bide his time, he wasn't willing to sit around while she went after another man she'd never even met.

If she wanted sex tonight, she was going to get it. But not with some stranger named Andre.

Hell, no.

She wanted Rayne. And he wanted her.

And it was time to satisfy them both.

7

"What the hell do you want?" asked the man who hauled open the door of Room 24. He was average-looking with short brown hair and a decent physique. He wore a pair of black slacks and a white dress shirt, the top button undone, the tails untucked.

"Maintenance," Rayne replied as he stared into the man's dark brown eyes and read all of his secrets.

Andre Martin was a thirty-three-year-old entertainment manager from Austin. Three times divorced. No kids. He routinely traveled the back roads of Texas with whichever band he was currently promoting in the Texas music market. This week it was a local group called the Lonestar Bad Boys. He'd met Robin Rivers during his last tour with the Boys. She'd been doing the drummer at the time, and anyone else who came along. She'd been his dream come true—a woman more interested in having fun than forging any sort of personal attachment.

After a trio of exes and a shitload of alimony, he'd been attracted to her immediately.

He'd had some of the hottest moments of his life with Rockin' Robin. She was a wildcat in the sack and he could only hope that the woman she'd recommended him to would be just as feisty.

If not, he would be okay with that, too. He'd popped a few Viagra just five minutes ago and he figured he had enough enthusiasm for the both of them.

Rayne's muscles clenched and his pulse kicked up a notch. He had half a mind to grab the man by the throat and kick his ass sixty ways to Sunday. But that wouldn't get him inside.

And if he wanted his plan to work, he had to get into this room.

He tamped down on his anger and added, "The hotel manager sent me to check a leak in the bathroom."

"Come back later." Andre started to close the door.

Rayne caught the doorjamb. While he couldn't cross the threshold without an official invitation, the door itself was in the middle. Fair game. "It'll just take a minute."

"Are you freakin' kidding me? I'm about to bust a nut, buddy. I don't have time for this crap."

"You better make time or the only thing busting in this room is going to be a pipe." He glanced past the man into the cheesy motel room. "This place is bad enough dry. I doubt you'll win any brownie points if your lady friend has to wade in water up to her kneecaps."

It was enough to make Andre think. He glanced at his watch. "Oh, all right. Come in, but make it fast."

Rayne followed the man into the small motel room.

"The bathroom's thataway." Andre motioned to a narrow archway.

"And your car's that way." Rayne indicated the open door. "Why don't you get the hell out of here?"

Andre frowned. "What the hell—" he started, but the words quickly stalled. His gaze widened and then it was as if a lightbulb flicked off. His expression went blank, his mouth slack.

"You're going to leave now," Rayne told him, "and forget all about me. I was never here, and neither was anyone else. The lady stood you up. You waited for her, but she never showed. Now get your shoes and leave."

The man nodded, snatched up his discarded loafers and left the small room. Hinges creaked. The door slammed. A few seconds later, a car engine caught. Tires spewed gravel and Andre was gone.

Rayne walked over to the dresser and fingered the tie the man had left behind. It was a red pin-striped number that smelled of expensive men's cologne and a heady dose of lust.

An idea struck and a grin tugged at the corner of Rayne's mouth. He'd planned to close the blinds and kill the lights, but the tie would work even better.

Hooking the piece of silk around his neck, he kicked off his boots, sank into a nearby chair and settled in to wait.

LUCY EYED THE FADED 24 hanging on the front of the motel door and knocked for the fifth time before glancing at her watch.

She was ten minutes late because she'd had to stop off for gas. The pay-at-the-pump card slot hadn't worked so she'd had to go inside. There she'd gotten stuck talking to old man Quinby, who worked the register every evening because Medicare didn't pay him enough to buy a pot to piss in (his exact words). She'd gotten an earful about Barney Colby's new tractor and Melvin Doolittle's hearing aid and Amos Culpepper's hemorrhoids before she'd managed to escape back to her car.

Maybe he'd given up on her and left.

She turned and took a quick visual of the parking lot. Other than a small red truck that sat near the lobby, her Saturn was the only other car in the lot. Relief bubbled inside her.

Wait a second. Relief? She wanted to do this.

If she didn't, she knew she would end up in bed with Rayne Montana faster than she could blink.

Worse, she would end up in love with him.

Again.

She drew a deep breath, forced aside her reservations and knocked again. Maybe he was the one running late. He could have gone out for champagne or strawberries or something.

Not that she needed champagne or strawberries or anything remotely romantic. This was sex. Pure and simple.

Survival.

She reached for the knob. The latch clicked and the door creaked open.

"Hello?" she called out, but no one answered.

She ignored the butterflies in her stomach, forced her feet to move, and walked into the small motel room. She'd barely made it three steps before she heard the deep voice.

"What took you so long?"

"Me? I've been knocking for ages—" She started to turn, but strong hands came up on either side of her and a hard, muscular chest pressed against her shoulder blades as he stepped up behind her.

"Don't," he murmured as he pulled her back firmly against him.

The door shut with a solid thud. Darkness closed in

around them and she became acutely aware of the press of his arousal between her buttocks. A tiny thrill chased away her doubt, but then his arms came from behind and he lifted a red silk tie to her eyes. The doubts rushed back full force.

She caught his hands. "W-what are you doing?"

"Making things interesting," he murmured, his voice deep and raw and oh so seductive. "The less we know about each other, the better." His lips brushed the shell of her ear. "Isn't that what you want, sugar?"

It was exactly what she wanted. No strings. No complications. No connection.

At the same time, she couldn't escape the strange current that hummed in the air and sizzled across her nerve endings. A familiar feeling that filled her with a generous dose of déjà vu. As if she'd touched and been touched by him before.

Right.

They were strangers to one another.

The only thing remotely familiar to this scene was the seedy motel room. While she'd never been in this particular one, she'd seen more than her share of look-alikes over the years. The outdated shag carpet. The paisley print bedspread. The quarter slot on the bedpost.

That was what made it all seem as if she'd been there, done that. It certainly wasn't the man standing behind her, filling up all of her breathing space.

She dropped her hands and the material slithered over her eyes. Strong fingers grazed her cheeks as he secured the silk and fastened a knot at the nape of her neck. A quick tug confirmed that it was secure.

Her stomach did a somersault and her hands trembled.

Despite her extensive resumé when it came to men, she'd never been blindfolded before. Most of her past encounters—while plenty—had been fast and no frills, the men much too excited to climb into bed with the infamous Lucy Rivers to be the slightest bit adventurous. They'd always been more concerned with taking their own pleasure than giving any in return. Once they'd gotten their groove on, they'd walked away.

It would be the same this time.

The notion stirred a ripple of regret that she gladly ignored by shifting her attention to the man standing so close to her.

With her vision gone, she had to focus on her other senses. Her ears tuned to the distinct sounds. The rustle of denim as he rounded her. The creak of a floorboard as he planted himself in front of her. The thunder of her own heart as she waited.

He took her hands, pulling her forward a few steps and steering her around before he let go.

"Lift your arms." His deep voice caused awareness to sizzle across her nerve endings.

She did as he commanded, her breath paused, her heart pounding.

She waited to feel the press of a hand or the brush of fingers as he started to undress her, but there was nothing. It was as if the clothes peeled away all by themselves.

Her tank top glided up and over her head. The button tugged and twisted at her waistband before sliding free. The zipper hissed and the shorts crept down her legs.

When the denim pooled at her ankles, she stepped free wearing nothing but her cowboy boots. She bent to pull them off, but his voice stopped her.

"Don't. I want to see you. Just like that."

She straightened and simply stood there. The cool air chugging from a nearby window unit whispered across her bare arms, her shoulder blades, her breasts, the very tips of her throbbing nipples. The seconds ticked by and she couldn't help but wonder what he was thinking.

Not that it mattered.

This wasn't about what he thought of her. What he felt.

It was all about what she felt. The heat. The desperation. The lust.

That was what she told herself, but she hesitated anyway. While she'd agreed to this—she needed this—she couldn't escape the feeling that something wasn't right.

She retreated, coming up hard against the edge of the bed.

"Easy." He caught her before she pitched backward. His strong hands steadied her, fingertips cool and soothing on her flushed skin.

"Trust me—" her voice trembled as fiercely as her aroused body "—there's nothing easy about this." The words rushed out before she could stop them. She drew a deep breath and tried to calm her pounding heart. "I don't mean to be so skittish. It's just that I've been on the wagon for quite some time now when it comes to sex. I don't usually do things like this anymore."

"Why not?"

She wasn't sure what prompted her to answer him rather than tell him to mind his own business. Maybe it was the blindfold. Maybe it was the fact that she didn't know him and he didn't know her and, therefore, wouldn't be around to judge her later. Maybe it was the sincerity in his voice, as if he really, really wanted to know.

Maybe all three.

Either way, the truth slipped past her lips before she could stop it. "I want more than just a physical relationship with a man. I want to go out to dinner and cuddle up in front of the TV. I want something real. This—" she shook her head "—this is meaningless."

"This, darlin'," he murmured after a long, silent moment, "is as real as it gets." He slid an arm around her and touched the small of her back. As if to prove his words, he bent her backward and the wet heat of his mouth closed over one throbbing nipple. A wave of delicious pleasure swept through her.

He suckled her with an expertise that made her sag against him. Wetness flooded the sensitive flesh between her legs and she felt a drop glide down the inside of her thigh.

He drew on her harder, his jaw creating a powerful tugging that she felt clear to her core. An echoing throb started in her belly, more intense with every rasp of his tongue, every pull of his delicious mouth.

But there was something else, as well.

A sharp, prickling sensation against her skin that tickled and stirred and ahhhhhhhhhh....

She slid her arms around his neck and held on tight. Heat flowered through her, pulsed along her nerve endings, and upped her body temperature until she felt as if she were about to go up in flames.

A gasp parted her lips as he left one breast throbbing and worked his way to the other. He drew on her so fast and fierce that she had to cling to him to keep her legs from giving out.

She felt the prickling again. Like something sharp scraping against her sensitive flesh. On either side of her nipple. The underside of her breast. The very tip. Goose bumps chased up and down her arms. Awareness skittered up her spine, along with a ripple of—uh, oh.

A vision lit up the darkness and she saw herself standing behind the Iron Horseshoe with Rayne Montana. She felt his lips on hers, felt the prickling against her mouth, tasted the blood—

Wait a second. Wait. Just. A. Friggin'. Second.

First off, this wasn't Rayne. This guy wasn't even close. Sure, he had a great mouth and he knew how to use it, but it wasn't the greatest. Her imagination was getting the best of her because of Rayne's sudden appearance and her deprived hormones.

She hadn't even kissed him last night, and he sure as hell hadn't bitten her. She'd bitten her own lip in her haste to get away from him.

"You're wet." His raw words slid into her ears and drew her full attention. She felt his touch on the inside of her thigh as he caught a drop of her essence. The rough pad of his finger slid higher, gathering the moisture until he poised at her entrance.

Her breath caught and she waited, hoping to feel him closer, deeper.

He drew his hand away and regret wiggled through her. But then she heard his deep, throaty moan. A split second later, he was kissing her again.

She tasted her own ripe sweetness on his lips and her insides clenched. Time pulled her back to the old barn that sat behind Rayne's run-down house.

She felt the soft hay beneath her bare feet. The rich aroma of leather and aroused male filled her nostrils. The sound of her own frantic breathing blended with the whisper of the wind and the buzz of crickets. Rayne stood in front of her, his arms around her, his mouth covering hers, coaxing her.

And while she would never fall into bed with the man himself, there suddenly seemed nothing wrong with tumbling head over heels into a fantasy of him.

Her reservations melted and Lucy did what she'd wanted to do so desperately last night—she slid her arms around his neck and kissed him for all she was worth.

8

SHE TASTED SO DAMNED GOOD.

The thought echoed through his head as his tongue darted into his mouth and she kissed him for all she was worth. Deeply. Thoroughly. Until his body clenched and his gut twisted.

He couldn't help himself. He needed more of her. Now.

He steered her down onto the bed. Leaning over her, he pushed her thighs as far apart as he could. He parted her with his thumbs and rasped her with his tongue. He licked her, plying her soft, swollen tissue, drawing the sensitive heart of her into his mouth and drinking in her ripe sweetness. She arched against him, her hips lifting off the bed, searching for more.

He knew that, not because he was a vampire and could see her every thought. Because he couldn't—not while she wore a blindfold. Rather, he read the desperation in the rapid rise and fall of her luscious breasts, the frantic gasp that parted her full pink lips, the way she lifted her hips and arched into his mouth.

She clutched the sheets and threw her head back. A cry burst from her lips and an orgasm gripped her voluptuous body.

He felt the rush of warmth against his tongue and tasted her sweet, vibrant energy. He soaked it up, licking and sucking and holding her close until the last spasm subsided and she went limp, her legs spread wide, her body spent.

Easing back, he stared at her for a long moment and relished the sight of her before his appetite reminded him that it wasn't nearly satisfied. He unzipped his jeans and shoved them down. His erection sprang forward, hot and pulsing.

Old habits died hard and he fished a condom from his pants pocket. Ripping it open, he rolled the latex onto his cock. His fingertips brushed the engorged head and a hiss sizzled past his lips. Hunger gnawed at him, pushing and pulling at his insides.

He settled himself between her legs, arms braced on either side of her, his hot erection pressed against her damp cleft. She was so wet and warm, and Rayne forgot all about the soft touches and seductive petting he engaged in with most women. The more turned on they were, the fiercer the climax.

But this was different. This was Lucy and suddenly the need to be inside her preceded everything.

His first thrust was deep and urgent. Light exploded behind his eyes and his heart seemed to stop. Her body felt so soft and slick and right.

The thought struck just as she lifted her hips to draw him in a fraction deeper. Pleasure, hot and acute, rushed through him and for the next few moments he forgot all about the demon that now lived and breathed inside him. Time sucked him back and instead of the hunger, he felt the pure, bone-deep ecstasy of being with Lucy Rivers.

He thrust into her again, fast, furious, desperate. He kept going, pounding over and over until his own climax hit him like a freight train. His muscles bunched. His body tightened. Before he could stop himself, his lips pulled back, his fangs tingled and a fierce cry rumbled up his throat.

Lucy froze, her hands going to the blindfold.

"No," he growled. He caught her wrists and pinned them above her head.

"But something's wrong—"

He pressed his mouth to hers and silenced the rest of her words. She tasted so sweet and he ached to sink his fangs into her bottom lip, to feel the spurt of blood as it rushed over his tongue and burned down his throat and—

No!

He shot to his feet. Yanking on his clothes, he hit the door as fast as his vampire speed could carry him.

As much as she made him feel like just a man when he was in her arms, he knew better. He felt the beast eating away inside him, demanding more. His body trembled and his hands shook. It was all he could do to make it around the side of the building to his pickup and haul open the door before it was too late.

Before he sank his fangs into her sweet flesh and drank his fill—the way he had that first time when he'd all but killed that poor woman outside a village in Kabul.

He'd tasted the first few drops and he'd been out of control. An animal. A murderer.

All the more reason for him to finish his business in Skull Creek and get the hell out. Before the bloodlust got the best of him and he finally lost complete control.

He intended to be far, far away from anyone when that happened again.

Shoving the truck into gear, he peeled out of the parking lot and hauled his hungry ass in the opposite direction.

LUCY PUSHED THE blindfold from her eyes just as the peel of tires echoed in her head.

What the…?

She glanced around the cheap motel room, her gaze searching for some sign of him. His boots tossed on the floor. Jeans in a pile. Shirt hooked over the back of a chair.

Nothing.

It was if she'd just imagined the entire encounter.

Except for her body.

Her nipples ached from being sucked. Her skin tingled from the rasp of his fingertips. Her clitoris pulsed from the stroke of his erection as he'd plunged into her.

She tossed back the sheet. Heat fired her cheeks as she pushed to her feet. She stumbled to the nearest window just as the grumble of the engine faded. Catching the edge of the shade, she pushed it aside and stared through the dingy glass. The motel signed buzzed near the road, the VACANCY light shining in bright green letters, illuminating the gravel parking lot. Wispy white dust lingered in the air, settling on the hood of her small red Saturn that sat nearby. There was no sign of a second vehicle. A motorcycle. Not even a bicycle.

Because he's long gone.

Her chest tightened and her eyes burned and she stiffened.

So what if he'd left already? It wasn't as if she'd wanted to have an actual conversation with the guy. She had to be up early tomorrow. She was buying a new blanket for Miss Wilma to replace the one Dr. Jekyll, aka Cupid, had destroyed a few days ago. After that, she had to head into work early to do some inventory for Zeke before the Horseshoe opened at lunchtime.

She didn't have time for small talk.

Still…he could have at least said something. "It was nice." "I enjoyed it." Something.

She forced her hand away and flipped on a nearby lamp. Pulling on her discarded clothes, she tried to ignore the crazy disappointment that whispered through her.

She should be happy right now. Ecstatic. Relieved.

She'd given in to her traitorous hormones, which meant she could face Rayne Montana without the overwhelming urge to jump his bones.

Holding tight to the hope, Lucy pulled on her clothes, snatched up her purse and headed back to town.

There would be no more lewd thoughts or wet dreams or erotic fantasies.

She was good to go. Back in control. Satisfied.

SHE WASN'T EVEN CLOSE to being satisfied.

Lucy admitted that much when she finally turned into her driveway a half hour later. Her hands shook and her skin tingled and she felt as anxious as when she'd first pulled up at the motel.

She tried to ignore the strange feelings as she let Cupid out in the backyard to get a little exercise and turned her attention to what was left of her laundry room. She swept up the dog food he'd spilled and threw out the blouse he'd shredded. And the pillowcase. And a pair of her favorite jeans.

But no matter how hard she worked or how many ingenious deaths she plotted for the mean little dog, she couldn't seem to distract herself from the memories.

They stayed with her, keeping her nerves on edge and her body primed.

She tried everything she could think of to unwind—a glass of warm milk and meditation and even a few hours of mindless infomercials. Nothing helped. Instead, she wound up buying two juicers off the QVC and a night cream guaranteed to stave off crow's-feet for another twenty years.

By the time she finally relaxed enough to doze off, it was almost daybreak.

Cupid woke her up an hour later with several sharp barks.

"Just be quiet for a half hour," she grumbled as she forced her eyes open and glared at the dog that perched on the end of the bed. "Please. I'll give you anything you want. Just name it. An extra jerky treat. A rawhide strip. My first born." The animal wagged its tail and dipped its nose. That was when Lucy noticed the small pink pillow at Cupid's feet.

The pillow was the result of her first home-economics assignment. Since she hadn't had any money to buy real material, she'd cut up an old party dress she'd bought for a quarter at the local Salvation Army. The result had earned her first A ever and it had been the first time she'd felt really proud of herself.

She'd wanted to be a designer from that moment on.

Cupid growled and nuzzled the pillow and Lucy knew immediately what the dog had in mind. "Don't even think about it."

Cupid dropped the pink sequined square and stepped on the edges with both paws. He let loose a tell-tale growl and eyeballed the pillow.

"I mean it." Lucy struggled upright and reached for the stuffed memento, but Cupid was faster. The animal snatched it up, threw it to the floor and pounced. Fabric ripped and stuffing flew.

"Noooooooo!" Lucy scrambled from the bed and hit the floor on all fours, but it was too late. The pillow was a shredded mess. "That's it. You're dead meat."

"I knew it," a voice declared from a nearby window.

Lucy glanced up from her hands and knees to see Eileen Warner from the local animal shelter peering in the open window, a clipboard in hand. "Need I remind you that death threats violate the ninth code of the Skull Creek Animal Shelter Bill of Animal Rights."

"I wasn't threatening him. I was just—"

"Trying to get him to quiet down by whatever means necessary in order to catch a few more minutes of sleep? You have a dog now, Miss Rivers. A living, breathing creature that depends on you for everything. That is a hefty responsibility. Now if you're not up for it, I will be glad to take Cupid with me and find him a new owner—"

"I didn't mean to threaten him. It's just that he ripped up my—"

"That's what dogs do," Eileen cut in. "They chew on things and rip them up. Get used to it, or give up Cupid to someone who doesn't mind catering to the eccentric behavior of such a dear, sweet boy. I know a dozen people right now who would love to take him off your hands. I, myself, would even be willing to give him a good home. I've been meaning to get a dog of my own since Hank and I tied the knot. Our new house has a fenced-in backyard and everything." She shook her head. "I still can't believe Miss Moon left him to you in the first place. She worshipped that dog. It makes absolutely no sense at all."

To anyone but Lucy.

Miss M had been skeptical of Lucy's vow to turn her life around. The old woman had nagged and predicted failure. But when Lucy had scrimped and saved enough money to put the deposit down on her house, Miss M had finally been convinced. Lucy was, indeed, changing her life, and the old woman had been proud.

She hadn't said as much, of course. We're talking Miss M. But Lucy had arrived at her new home to find a huge fruit basket on her front steps and a note that read, You Can Do It.

She'd known the sender's identity right away. She'd also known that Miss M was trying to encourage her without blowing her own reputation for being an uppity hard ass, which was why she'd neglected to sign her name.

Still, Miss M had wanted her to succeed.

Which was why she'd given her Cupid.

Lucy glanced at the ball of fluff. He sat there looking like anything but the spawn of Satan. He wagged his tail and barked at her as if to say, "Let's play."

"He's such a sweet dog," Eileen remarked. "Anyone would be lucky to have him."

Lucy ignored the yapping dog, pushed to her feet and reached for her robe.

"Anyone, that is," Eileen went on, "but you." Her gaze

narrowed as she eyed Lucy. "It's obvious you can't handle him. Why don't you just admit that you're in over your head and—"

"Thanks so much for stopping by," Lucy cut in. She reached for the window. "But I've got it under control."

"That's not what it looked like to me—"

She shoved the glass down, threw the latch and pulled the curtains. Drawing a deep breath, she turned back and glared at the schizophrenic dog. "Look, I don't like you and you obviously don't like me, but we're stuck in this together so we might as well call a truce. You stay away from my stuff and I won't feed you to Zeke's German Shepherd. Agreed?"

The animal's response was to launch another attack on the one scrap of fabric that had survived the first offensive.

So much for making a deal with the devil.

Lucy reached down and pried the fabric from Cupid's mouth. She herded the animal into the backyard and then turned to what was left of her pillow. She blinked back the tears, steeled herself and gathered up the pieces.

She spent the rest of her morning hunched over her sewing machine, trying to stitch together the odds and ends. Cupid might have won the battle, but she fully intended to win the war. She wasn't giving up on him anymore than she was giving up on herself.

Nor was she picking up the phone again for another sex date with Andre.

No matter how much she suddenly wanted to.

9

HE WAS DYING. He knew that even though he could have sworn he'd been attacked just two days ago.

Or was it three?

He couldn't seem to quiet the pounding in his skull and sort through the strange images that filled his head. He just knew he was here on the side of some mountain. The quarter moon hung suspended in the sky, casting just enough light for him to see the narrow path that cut through the rough terrain.

Pain gripped his entire body. Clenching his muscles. Digging down deep and biting at his bones.

He stumbled forward, slamming into the rock walls that surrounded him as he wound his way down. Sharp edges sliced at his skin, but he didn't feel the warm dribble of blood. The terrorists who had attacked him had sucked him dry and he was all tapped out. Empty. Hungry.

A hallucination.

That was what he told himself. He was weak. Tired. He needed food and shelter and some much-needed sleep. Then his brain would clear and he could remember what really happened.

The pain. The blood. The death.

He slammed his mind shut to all three and forced his legs to move. Left. Right. Left. Right—

The silent orders slammed to a halt when he heard the sound of voices. He picked up his steps, pushing forward, expecting to find the source just around the next curve. The voices grew louder, more distinct, but there was no one there. He trudged on, gritting his teeth against what felt like a dull knife jabbing at his stomach. It would be so much easier to slow down. To give in.

To give up.

But he'd never given up.

Not when his mom had left him alone night after night to go hang out at the local bar. Not when his old man had beat the hell out of him after a drunken binge. Not back when he'd been captured by militants and tortured for three days during his first ops mission in Somalia. Not in any of the missions since.

Not ever.

Not now.

His stomach twisted and his legs screamed, but he forced another step. Then another. The voices blared in his head, along with a steady ka-thunk ka-thunk that sliced through the drum solo playing in his skull and forced his own pulse faster. He stumbled a few more steps and rounded a curve. The path faded into a thick stretch of trees.

He pushed on, ducking into the foliage. Branches scraped across his face and poked at his bare torso, but he kept moving. Just a little more...

The trees thinned and opened up into a small clearing. Small wood dwellings clustered here and there. A bonfire blazed in the very center. Even more, there were people.

Rayne felt a vise tighten in his gut. His hands shook and his mouth watered.

A soft voice pushed past the barrage of sounds and he turned to see an old woman standing behind him. Concern furrowed her brow as she stepped toward him and murmured in Arabic.

He knew her language as well as his own and there was no mistaking her distinct "Are you okay?"

He opened his mouth to answer, to explain his situation and ask for her help, but suddenly his mind went blank. The scent of warm, sweet blood filled his nostrils and his insides cramped. Something dark and deep swelled and a red haze clouded his vision.

A burst of energy rolled through him and he reached her just like that. He pressed her up against a tree and sank his teeth deep into her neck. Sweet, delicious life rushed into his mouth and poured down his throat and ecstasy washed through him. He sucked harder, taking and taking until—

RAYNE BOLTED UPRIGHT, his nerves buzzing, his muscles strung tight. He wiped a hand over his face and tried to erase the memories. The woman's helpless cry. Her old, withered hands struggling against him. The pain of a bullet ripping through his arm as the villagers spotted him and tried to save their own. The realization of what he'd almost done.

One more drop and she would have been dead.

Thanks to him.

He hadn't meant to turn on her, but the temptation had been far too great, her blood too potent, the beast too powerful in his weakened, confused state.

That was when Rayne had realized that he could never go back. Not to the Navy. To what was left of his family. To his life.

It was over. All he'd known. All he'd once been.

Over.

"Shit," he muttered, pushing to his feet.

He stalked over to the loft window and unlatched the old wood. The window creaked open. A soft breeze blew over his bare chest, but it didn't send so much as a shiver through him. A faint tinge of orange clung to the horizon, but not enough for him to shrink back. The sun had all but set. Shadows played across the pasture.

He drank in the details that he never would have noticed before—the way the grass seemed to sparkle in the last few rays of daylight, the sudden hush of insects as they waited for full darkness to descend, the rustle of a raccoon as it raced from the field to the edge of the nearby forest.

His gaze shifted to the old tractor that sat near the back of the house. Once upon a time it had been a shiny blue. Now it sat faded and rusted out, ready to crumble into a heap at the first serious gust of wind.

Rayne had spent half his youth on that tractor, plowing when his old man was too sloshed to stand up, much less operate a major piece of machinery, or just when he needed to shut out the doubts in his head. Demons that had told him he was every bit as worthless as his old man had said.

The tractor had been good at drowning out reality.

If only it could help him now.

He ducked through the window and poised on the ledge for a split second before leaping to the ground. He landed smoothly. No twinges of pain. No jolt to his muscles. Nothing.

He was a vampire now.

A goddamn vampire.

He started for the creek that ran at the far edge of the property. There'd been several rains in the past few weeks, so the water was over a foot deep. Rayne peeled off his clothes and waded out into the moving water. He sat down and let the cold liquid roll over his shoulders. It was the closest thing to a cold shower that he could think of without going inside the house, but it did little to cool the inferno that raged inside him. Nothing could quiet the hunger or the memories or the truth that he would have to feed again.

That he wanted to feed again.

Despite last night's sex.

Because of it.

While a little one-on-one was usually enough to sate him and send him looking for the next woman, it had been different with Lucy. The more he'd touched her, the more he'd wanted to touch her. The more he'd kissed her, the more he'd wanted to kiss her. The more he'd drank in her sweet orgasm, the more he'd wanted to drink from her.

Her body.

Her blood.

He hadn't, of course. He hadn't been that out-of-control.

Thanks to the blindfold.

With her eyes covered and her thoughts hidden, he'd been able to pretend that he was still the same man he'd once been and forget the monster he'd become.

The blindfold. That was what had made their encounter so different.

That and the fact that she wasn't just any woman. She was the only woman he'd ever loved. The woman he still loved.

And she loved him.

The thought stirred a tiny thrill. A crazy reaction because he knew it didn't make a damned bit of difference. The Realtor had already dropped off the paperwork. All he had to do was sign the papers and the sale would be complete.

He would sign.

First thing tomorrow.

Then he would walk away and leave Skull Creek for good.

But his leaving wouldn't hurt her this time because she hadn't known it was him. She thought she'd slept with some other guy.

And that was what she would think when he showed up for Round Two. Because Rayne intended to keep up the ruse.

Even if it did bother the hell out of him.

It was a small price to pay for one more memory to keep him company during all the dark, lonely nights that lay ahead.

10

SHE'D MADE IT.

Lucy gave herself a pat on the back as she shelved the last beer mug and called it a night. It was half past midnight and the bar had closed up shop thirty minutes ago. She'd not only managed to make a decent amount in tips thanks to Terence Green and his poker buddies, she'd also stayed a safe distance from the phone.

Luckily Rayne hadn't come into the bar during the six hours and thirty minutes she'd been battling her hormones. Otherwise, she had a sneaking suspicion she would have been a goner. But he'd steered clear of the Horseshoe and so she'd managed to stay on track.

She ignored a strange spiral of disappointment, grabbed her purse and told Zeke goodnight.

She was halfway through the parking lot when her skin prickled and awareness skittered up her spine.

She turned and drank in the empty stretch of gravel. The only light came from a single bulb that burned near the rear Exit. A Dumpster sat nearby, along with a stack of Corona boxes. She drew a deep breath and turned back around. Her car sat in the last row, next to Zeke's jacked-up 4x4 Chevy. Otherwise, the lot was empty. No extra cars. No visible stalkers.

She picked up her steps and hit the unlock button on her key fob. Climbing inside, she keyed the ignition and pulled out of the parking lot. But even inside her car, she couldn't escape the heat that skittered up and down her arms and the expectancy that sat in the pit of her stomach.

As if someone watched her.

Wanted her.

If only.

Turning on the radio, she found a lively country station and tried to distract herself from her traitorous body. It worked, too. By the time she pulled into her driveway, her breathing came a little easier and her heart had slowed to a steady beat.

But then she climbed out from the car and the feelings rushed back full-force. The frenzied nerves. The sizzle of electricity in the air. The knowledge deep in her gut that someone was nearby.

Her feet made quick work of the walkway and she mounted the steps, her key in hand. Wood creaked and she reached for the doorknob—

"Boo!"

Panic bolted through her. She whirled and the emotion faded in a rush of relief.

Robin stood behind her, a smile on her face.

"Jesus, you scared the crap out of me." Lucy forced a deep breath. She glanced at the empty driveway. "Where'd you come from?"

Robin indicated the swing that sat off to one side of the porch. "I'm waiting for my date. He's picking me up in a few minutes and I needed something to wear."

Lucy's gaze dropped to the familiar red and pink halter top that her sister wore. "Thanks for asking."

"Hey, you should be the one thanking me. That monster of yours would have shredded one of your couch cushions if I hadn't walked in and given him one of those doggy things to chew on."

Lucy glanced in the living-room window. Sure enough, Cupid sat in the center of the floor, gnawing on a rawhide strip. "But I left him in the laundry room."

"Maybe you forgot to close the door." Robin shrugged. "Or maybe he really does have special powers."

If only.

The only supernatural ability Cupid seemed to possess was the uncanny knack for destroying things.

At that moment, headlights rounded the corner.

"That's him," Robin quipped. "Gotta go." She started down the steps.

"Have fun," Lucy called after her.

Robin turned. "I'd say the same, but you won't do it. You're a great big chicken."

"What's that supposed to mean?"

"The Happy Trails Motel?" She signaled for her date to wait and arched an eyebrow at Lucy. "You chickened out."

"I did not."

Robin gave her a "yeah, right" look. "I ran into Andre last night at the new bar that just opened up over in Travis County. He told me he'd gotten stood up by a friend of mine. Since I don't make it a habit of recommending him to just anyone, I knew he was talking about you."

"Wait a second." Lucy eyed her sister. "You saw him? Last night?"

"Live and in color."

"What time?"

"About ten. He said he'd been waiting at the motel, but then you didn't show so he headed over to the bar to drown his disappointment. Poor guy."

"But that's impossible." At 10:00 p.m. she'd been engaged in the hottest sexual encounter of her life with Andre himself.

At least she'd thought it was him.

Shock gripped her as the reality of what her sister was telling her sank in.

She'd slept with the wrong man.

Or, in this case, the right man.

Memories rushed at her and her nostrils flared. She smelled the intoxicating scent of leather and raw male and a hint of danger. She heard the deep timbre of his voice. Felt the strong touch of his hand.

Oh, no.

"Are you okay?" Robin's concerned voice pushed past the panic thundering in Lucy's ears. She was next to her in an instant. "You don't look so good. Is something wrong?"

But it wasn't just something. It was everything. She'd done the unthinkable. She'd slept with Rayne Montana.

Rayne.

"Listen," Robin went on, her expression softening, "I know you're taking this celibacy thing seriously and I just want you to know that I think it's kind of cool."

"You do not."

"Okay, so I think it's kind of cool in a crazy, totally weird way, but that's only because it's not my personal choice. If it works for you, that's all that matters."

But it wasn't working at all. She'd not only fallen off the wagon, she'd done it with the one person she'd vowed not to sleep with.

It wasn't your fault. You didn't know.

The thing was, she had known. Deep inside, she'd recognized him, but she'd ignored the tell-tale signs and grasped at the fantasy because she hadn't wanted to stop. It had been so long and she'd missed him so much. She'd wanted to have sex with him.

She still did.

THE TRUTH HAUNTED HER as Robin and her date pulled out of the driveway a short while later and disappeared around the corner.

Lucy turned to open her front door. Her fingers clasped the knob. The door clicked open and a deep, seductive voice slid into her ears.

"I've been thinking about you." A hard male body stepped up behind her and every nerve went on instant alert. "About last night." Strong, muscular arms came around her and she saw the familiar red necktie dangling from his fingertips. "About this."

Her nipples tightened and anticipation coiled between her legs.

She wanted to have sex with him, all right.

Want.

It didn't have to go beyond that if she didn't let it. She was a grown woman, for heaven's sake. Experienced. Realistic.

Love did not equal sex. She knew that better than anyone.

Just as she knew Rayne would be leaving as soon as he

finished his business in Skull Creek. That was why he'd hidden his identity behind the blindfold. To keep things impersonal.

No ties. No complications.

He'd said so himself.

Regret niggled at her, but she forced it aside. Unlike years ago, she no longer had a young girl's illusions about the future.

She knew full well that they didn't have one.

They only had this moment.

And suddenly that seemed like enough.

"I've been thinking about you, too," she murmured. And then she caught his hands and guided the blindfold to her eyes.

11

HIS GUT CLENCHED and his body throbbed. He slid his arms around her waist, shoved his hands beneath her tank top and felt her bare skin. She was soft and warm and his body trembled. He picked her up, his lips eating at hers, but he couldn't cross the threshold.

"Can I come inside?"

"Yes," she breathed the invitation and anticipation coiled tighter.

"Say the words."

"Please," she murmured against his lips. "Come. Inside."

He carried her into the house and kicked the door shut. He bypassed a growling white fluff ball and headed down the hallway until he found what he was looking for.

The room looked like her, with its pale bedspread and soft colors. He didn't bother turning on the light. He didn't need to. Instead, he settled her on the bed and pulled back to reach for the button on his jeans. His fingers worked at the speed of light and in the blink of an eye, he shoved the denim down his legs.

He didn't lean into her and thrust his cock deliciously deep, however. Not yet. He wanted to look at her, to feast on the picture she made and stroke her soft skin and brand these next few moments into his head before the hunger gripped him and he could no longer think.

He closed his hands over her shoulders and guided her down onto the mattress. His fingers skittered over the soft material of her tank, molding the cotton to her ripe nipples and voluptuous breasts.

His fingers went to the button on her blue jean shorts. Lust whipped through him, gaining momentum with every pull and tug. His pulse quickened and an ache gripped him from the inside out. He stiffened, fighting the need that twisted his gut.

He smoothed the denim down her long, luscious legs. His fingertips brushed her bare skin, grazing and stirring and feeling.

His gaze traveled from her calves, up her lush thighs to the wispy lace covering the bare skin between her legs.

She was as smooth as a peach and his mouth went suddenly dry. Desire roared through him, fierce and demanding. Blood jolted through his veins. His hands seemed to move of their own accord then, traveling the length of her body, exploring every curve, every dip, lingering at the lace covering her sweet sex.

He traced the pattern with his fingertip before following the single strip of satin that ran between her legs and barely covered her slit. She gasped and her legs opened, causing a spiral of jealousy to shoot through him.

Because it wasn't him she opened for.

It was another man.

The truth gripped him for a long moment and sent a burst of desperation through him. Suddenly it wasn't about making his own memories, it was about making a place for himself in hers. About pleasuring her so that no matter how many encounters she had in the future, she would never forget this one night.

She would never forget him.

He dipped his finger beneath the satin and pushed into her steamy heat. Her full lips parted and her cheeks flushed. She arched her hips, rising up to meet him and draw him even more.

He sank a fraction deeper and leaned over her. His mouth closed over her nipple and he drew her in, suckling her hard for a long moment as he plunged his fingers deep. He eased the pressure with his mouth and hand to let her catch her breath and then he plunged back inside and sucked her in once again. Longer this time. Over and over. Until he felt the force of her release. Liquid warmth gushed from her sweltering center and drenched his fingers.

Electricity skimmed up his arm and spread through his body, igniting every nerve ending and chasing away the cold for several blissful seconds. Life pulsed through him and he vibrated with the energy of her climax.

IT WAS THE BEST ORGASM of Lucy's life.

The force of it lit up the darkness behind the blindfold, turning the black a vibrant collage of colors that made her almost dizzy. Heat licked at her and chased her breath away. Her body clenched and unclenched.

But it wasn't enough.

"Please." The desperate plea slid past Lucy's lips before she could stop herself.

A growl sizzled across her nerve endings as he urged

her legs even farther apart, pushed her into the mattress and settled his erection flush against her sex.

He kissed her then, licking her lips and sucking at her tongue before he caught her bottom and tilted her just so. With one powerful thrust he slid inside her.

The colors swimming behind her eyes burst into a brilliant white light as if lightning had just zapped her. The air stalled in her lungs and her heart seemed to stop as she forgot everything except the man filling her up.

Her body arched into him and she grasped at his shoulders. He thrust again, pushing deeper this time—every time—and creating the most delicious friction until she couldn't take it anymore. Ecstasy crashed over her, picking her up and rocking her back and forth for a long, breathless moment.

Through the ringing in her own ears, she heard his deep groan and suddenly she couldn't help herself. She wanted to see him.

She needed to.

He bucked inside her, his body going rigid. He thrust deep one last time and she shoved the blindfold from her eyes.

He was poised above her, his arms braced on either side. His muscles bulged. His skin glistened with perspiration. His jaw clenched. A growl vibrated in her ears. His mouth fell open and his fangs gleamed in the dim light and—

She blinked, but he didn't disappear. They didn't disappear.

"Rayne?" His name trembled from her lips and he went ramrod stiff.

His eyes snapped open. His gaze shimmered a hot,

vibrant purple and as she stared deep, her panic subsided. She forgot that no way in heaven, hell or the in between could this really be happening. She couldn't be seeing purple eyes because Rayne had aqua-blue eyes. Aqua. And he certainly didn't have fangs.

Instead, she forgot all the questions and simply felt the rightness of the moment. Because she was meant for him and he was meant for her and…

Forever.

FOREVER?

The word blared in Rayne's head and zapped him back to reality. To the all-important fact that he was staring down at Lucy, reading her every thought, and she was staring back up at him, lost in the magic of his gaze. And he was this close to dipping his head and sinking his teeth into her sweet neck.

Holy shit.

He tore himself away from her and stumbled backward, releasing her from his spell. His back came up hard against the opposite wall and sheetrock cracked. His gut twisted. His body shook.

One drink, the hunger whispered. *Just one and it won't hurt so much.*

But one wouldn't be enough. He'd want another. And another. Until he'd feasted on every drop and there was nothing left.

His stomach clenched and his muscles contorted. His mouth watered and his fangs ached. His gaze riveted on her lush body and an invisible hand tightened around him and squeezed.

Until the pain grew unbearable. Suddenly, everything faded into a red haze and just like that, the battle was over.

He'd resisted long enough.

He needed blood. And he needed it now.

RAYNE'S EYES BLAZED a bright, furious red and shock snatched up Lucy and refused to let go. His teeth pulled back and his fangs glittered and fear spiraled through her.

Along with a ripple of anticipation.

"I'm sorry." The deep, anguished voice echoed in her ears, but his mouth didn't move.

Because he wasn't actually talking. He was inside her head. A vampire.

No!

She clamped her eyes shut. The bed shifted as he leaned down. This was it. The end.

Or the beginning.

The thought struck and then faded in the groan of mattress springs and the slam of a door.

Her eyes popped open to find the room empty. Footsteps echoed down the hallway and the front door slammed.

Thankfully.

She could still see the tortured look on his face, the blazing red eyes, the fangs.

Real, honest-to-goodness fangs.

She wouldn't have believed it if she hadn't seen it with her own eyes. Even now, she wasn't one-hundred-percent certain and her mind raced for a more plausible explanation. The room was too dark and she hadn't seen clearly. Or maybe the blindfold had caused some sort of optic reaction that had her seeing lights and shadows and him.

That was what she told herself, but deep down she knew the truth.

She'd known that night at the bar when she'd spotted him for the first time after all these years. He'd looked the same, but he'd felt different. He'd had an intensity about him that hadn't been there before. A strength that had seeped into her and stirred the most provocative images.

Or so she'd thought.

She'd dismissed the cut lip and the strange thoughts as her overactive imagination, but they'd been real. Those moments in the back alley had been real. He'd been real.

A bloodsucker.

A vampire.

The word echoed in her head, along with the roar of an engine. But suddenly the truth didn't bother her half as much as the notion that she would never see him again.

She wouldn't.

The knowledge crystallized as she rushed to the window and watched his truck disappear down the road.

Relief. That was what she should be feeling at this moment. That and pure joy because she was still alive and breathing.

Instead emptiness settled in the pit of her stomach. Regret slithered around her and yanked tight.

Because Rayne Montana was gone again and she knew as surely as she knew that she still loved him, that there was no coming back this time.

12

RAYNE SWERVED into the parking lot of the Qwick Pick and slammed on the brakes. It wasn't a crowded bar or a busy diner, but it would do.

She would do.

He stared through the window at the girl who stood behind the counter. She wore a paisley print handkerchief tied around her head à la Axl Rose from Guns N' Roses, a Qwick Pick name tag and a bored expression.

Rayne wanted to see more, to catch her attention and stare into her eyes, but that would take too long and he couldn't wait.

He could only feel. The pain eating him up. The hunger yawning inside. The bloodlust roaring through his veins.

Now.

In the blink of an eye, he stood in front of her. Her surprised gaze caught his a split second before he reached over the counter.

"What the hell, mister—" The words faded into a choked gurgle as he caught her by the throat and pulled her forward.

He heard the frantic staccato of her heart, smelled the rich, ripe scent of her blood. Both were like a drug and he was a junkie who'd gone too long without.

"Don't do it." The deep voice was like an ice pick penetrating the roar in his ears.

But Rayne couldn't stop on his own.

He growled, lowering his mouth, his lips closing around her throat as he sank his fangs deep. The first few drops touched his tongue, but it wasn't ecstasy that bolted through him.

Pain exploded in his skull. He released the clerk and stumbled backward. He whirled and his vision shook. Through the blur, he caught sight of a man wearing jeans and a T-shirt that read, Save a Horse, Ride a Cowboy. A pair of blazing-red eyes met his and shock jolted him.

His legs gave out and he slammed into the floor. His head snapped back. A knifelike sensation sliced through the base of his skull.

And then the lights went out.

"NOT AGAIN," Lucy cried, staring at the mess that had once been her laundry room.

The giant-size box of laundry detergent she'd bought at the local Walmart had been shredded and it looked as if a blizzard had erupted inside the small room. The plastic laundry basket had been chewed within an inch of its life and her favorite jeans, which had been hanging on a nearby rack, were now in a shredded pile. It was just past midnight and she'd spent the past hour trying to convince herself that what she'd seen and heard had been a great big figment of her imagination.

The result of desperate hormones.

And an overloaded work schedule.

And the stress of having a dog possessed by the devil himself.

Her gaze riveted on Cupid, who stood atop what was left of the jeans, his tail wagging, his tongue lolling. "You're supposed to be helping me, not making my life a living hell."

The dog flipped onto his back and did a quick twist as if pleased with his efforts.

"I should call Ellen," she declared. "And hand you over."

But she wouldn't. She knew that and so did Cupid. She needed him now more than ever because her love life totally sucked.

Literally.

A vampire.

A tiny part of her brain still protested the truth, even though she knew deep inside it was true. She couldn't forget the stroke of his fingers up and down the beer bottle and how she'd felt the touch directly on her back. The frown on his face when she'd called Andre, as if he'd heard her proposition across the crowded, noisy bar.

He had heard. Just as he'd touched her.

Just as he'd come this close to sucking her blood tonight.

Regret wiggled through her for a split second before she reminded herself that she didn't want him to suck her blood.

Nor did she want to know what had happened to him to turn him from the man he'd once been to the vampire that he was now.

Had he been attacked? Had he crossed over willingly?

She shook her head. She wasn't going to think about the dozens of questions that raced through her mind or the fact that she would never know the answer to any of them. Now more than ever she needed to do what she should have done years ago—forget Rayne once and for all and get on with her life.

Reaching for the dustpan, she spent the next fifteen minutes cleaning up Cupid's mess.

And then she did the only thing she could think of—she grabbed the dog, crawled back into bed with him, and cried herself to sleep.

WHERE THE HELL WAS HE?

Rayne swept a gaze around the large windowless bedroom. The walls were paneled in dark oak, the floor a gleaming, polished wood. A large plasma TV hung on one wall and a kick-ass stereo system filled the shelves on the adjacent wall. Above him, the rafters were open with dark beams criss-crossing, making the room seem larger than it actually was.

He pushed against the soft king-size mattress and tried to sit up, but his head hurt too damned much. He closed his eyes against the throbbing and forced his brain to do a rewind.

It took a few seconds, but slowly the memories started to replay.

He saw Lucy staring up at him. Heard her shocked gasp. Felt the beast take control.

Fast-forward to the Qwick Pick. He'd been about to rip the throat out of the clerk, to sink his fangs deep and taste her sweet, sweet blood and then…

He shook his head, trying to push aside the throbbing

pain and think. He needed to see everything. To know what had happened. What he'd done.

"Don't do it." The deep voice echoed in his head and he saw the man.

"You're awake."

The deep voice pulled him from his thoughts. Rayne blinked and focused on the man standing in the open doorway. It was the same man from the convenience store. He looked to be in his late twenties. Tall. Toned. Blond. He wore the same T-shirt and worn jeans and a calm expression, as if he wasn't the least bit afraid Rayne would find his strength and attack.

"Sorry I had to knock you out, but I didn't have a choice. As frenzied as you were, it was the only way to get you out of the store before you committed a major felony."

The truth shattered the throb in his skull and Rayne's gaze widened.

He actually smiled then. "I know you're some hotshot Navy SEAL, but you weren't yourself a few hours ago. You were hungry, and that makes the best of us extremely stupid."

"Who are you?"

"Not who. What."

Rayne shook his head and tried to make some sense out of what was happening. The hunger still coiled inside him, clenching at his insides, making it hard to really focus. "What's that supposed to mean?"

"Don't you know?" His gaze narrowed as he stared at Rayne. "You don't know, do you? How old are you?"

"Thirty-two."

"I mean when were you turned into a vampire?"

Surprise skittered up Rayne's spine, quickly replaced by

a rush of shock when he saw the strange shimmer in the man's gaze. Realization crashed down around him and his head hurt that much more. "Holy shit. You're a vampire."

"The fact that you didn't know tells me you can't be more than a month or so old."

Panic bolted through Rayne and every cell in his body screamed for him to get the hell out of here. Now.

At the same time, his instincts—the ones that had saved his ass time and time again overseas—told him this vampire posed no threat. If so, he would have killed Rayne while he was unconscious and vulnerable.

"Two weeks," he heard himself rasp. The effort made his jaw throb. His throat burned and he tried to swallow.

"That explains it then."

"What?" he croaked.

"Why you didn't feel me in the store. That and the fact that you were out of your head with hunger. How long has it been since you fed?"

"Last night."

The man gave him a knowing look. "I'm talking blood, not sex."

"Almost two weeks."

"No wonder you flipped. You're lucky I was driving by. I knew there was a new vampire in town, but I didn't know who you were until I saw you get out of the truck. I smelled the frenzy and I knew you were about to go over the edge." The vampire shrugged. "Don't worry. It happens to the best of us. You just have to learn how to deal with it."

But Rayne didn't want to deal with it. He wanted to forget. Forget the beast gnawing inside him. The blood on his hands. The realization of what he'd done.

He'd almost attacked Lucy.

"The name's Cody. Cody Braddock."

"Rayne Montana."

"I already knew who you were." He indicated the dog tags sitting on the nightstand before holding up two plastic packets. "Here." He tossed them at Rayne. "I poured some down your throat last night to calm you down, but it wasn't nearly enough. You need more."

An image rushed at Rayne, of the blood streaming into his mouth and easing the pain for a few blessed moments.

"Drink up," Cody added.

Rayne stared at the bags of sustenance and hunger sucker punched him. His fangs throbbed. Desperation rushed through him. Before he could stop himself, he punctured one of the plastic bags with his teeth and inhaled the sweet ambrosia. It filled his mouth and warmed his throat and he felt his muscles relax.

"Where did you get this?" he gasped when he finally finished the first packet. He set it on the nightstand while his other hand tightened on the second, like a starving man holding onto the last piece of bread.

"One of us has connections to a blood bank in Austin."

"Us? You mean there are more?"

"Skull Creek has several vampires." Cody shook his head. "You would have known that if you hadn't been so starved. It's one of our powers. We can sense each other. Detect friend or foe. It helps make up for the fact that we can't read another vampire's mind. That only works with humans. We can do a whole shitload of other things, as well, but we'll talk about that later, when you can think a little more clearly. Drink," he said, turning on his heel.

"I have to head out for a little while, but I'll be back before daybreak."

"What time is it?"

"About 3:00 a.m. You should go ahead and get some sleep. You can stay here today. This evening you can meet the others."

But Rayne didn't plan on sticking around long enough to meet anyone. Just because there were others like him didn't change the fact that he'd almost killed Lucy last night.

He would have because once he sank his fangs deep, he could no longer think. The beast took control and forced him to do the unthinkable.

He wouldn't put her in that kind of danger.

She'd turned her back on him for his own good the last time, so that he could have the kind of life he'd always wanted. It was his turn to return the favor.

Rayne waited until he heard a door close overhead and a truck start, and then he forced his legs over the side of the bed. Pulling on his boots, he pushed to his feet, shoved the second bag of blood into his back pocket and headed back to his place.

A few signatures and he was out of here for good.

13

"WE HAVE TO TALK," Miranda declared when she barged in and interrupted Lucy's pity party an hour later.

Lucy stared at her youngest sister standing in the bedroom doorway before glancing at the clock on the nightstand. "It's four in the morning. Don't you think whatever it is can wait until tomorrow?"

"There's something I need to tell you." Her gaze collided with Lucy's. "It's about Cody."

Lucy's misery faded in a rush of panic and she struggled to a sitting position. "Don't tell me he broke up with you."

"Of course not. It's not about us. It's just about him. Now I know this is going to sound strange, but I need you to work with me on this." She stopped pacing and stared at Lucy. "Cody's not just a retired bull rider."

"Okay, so he's not a retired bull rider. So what?"

"I didn't say he wasn't a retired bull rider. I said he's not just a retired bull rider. He's more."

"A construction worker? A poet? What?"

"A vampire. I know it's crazy and unbelievable—" she rushed on before the words could fully sink in "—and I don't expect you to believe me, but it's true. I haven't told you because I didn't want to freak you out. You're not freaked out, are you?" She waved a hand and blurted, "Stupid question. Of course, you're freaked out. You probably think I've flipped my lid, but I swear it's true. Vampires do exist and Cody is one. In fact, there are several others right here in Skull Creek. There's Cody's brother, Brent. He's a vampire. And Jake and Dillon and Garret over at Skull Creek Choppers—they're all vampires. And Garret's wife. She's an ancient vampire. And, well, I just want you to know that it's not the end of the world that Rayne is a vampire—"

"I know."

Miranda did a double take. "You do?"

"We were..." The words trailed off as she remembered their lovemaking. Her eyes watered. "He was here tonight and we were sort of together."

Miranda arched an eyebrow. "Sort of as in a movie and popcorn? Or sort of as in, Oh, baby?"

"Number two," she admitted. "One minute he was fine and the next his eyes changed colors and he grew fangs."

"And?"

"And nothing. He realized I was looking at him and he left."

"He didn't bite you?" When Lucy shook her head, Miranda added, "No wonder he was in such bad shape when Cody found him."

Panic bolted through her. "What are you talking about?"

"Cody found him at the Qwick Pick, half-starved and out of control." She shook her head. "I can't believe he didn't bite you."

"Who cares about that? Is he okay?"

She nodded. "Cody saved him and gave him a few bags of blood that he gets from some blood bank in Austin." She smiled. "It comes in handy once in a while. Especially for a new vampire. It can help him learn to control the hunger so he doesn't feel so frenzied. He can learn to pace himself and basically live a somewhat normal life. After hours, that is. But I'm getting ahead of myself, aren't I? I should probably slow down and let you digest all of this."

Exactly, but her mind was still stuck on Rayne and the fact that he'd been sick. Starved.

"He's at Cody's place?"

"Not anymore. Cody left him to come and pick me up, but by the time we got back, he was gone. That's when we came here. We thought you would want to know what happened." She stared at her sister for a long moment. "You let him go once without a fight. You aren't making the same dumb mistake again, are you?"

"I had to let him go. He never would have been happy stuck here. He would have blamed me every day for standing in his way."

"But he came back," Miranda pointed out.

"Only to sell his place."

"He could have done that long distance. He came back for you, Lucy. Can't you see that?"

"Did he say something to Cody?"

"He didn't have to. He obviously loves you, otherwise he never would have found the strength to pull away from you tonight. Trust me, feeding is everything for a new vampire."

"Unless he's in love." The comment came from the handsome man who appeared in the doorway. "He found the strength to resist what he is because of you. Because you're the one."

Cody's words echoed in Lucy's head and for a split second, she actually believed them. She'd seen the struggle on Rayne's face. It had killed him to pull away tonight. But he'd done it anyway.

Because he loved her?

"Exactly," Cody said, and Lucy's eyes widened. He shrugged. "One of the perks of being a vampire. I can read your thoughts."

"If you let him," Miranda added. "But you can keep him out if you want to. All you have to do is focus and, bam, instant privacy. It's like a wall going up." She must have noted the tremble of Lucy's lips, because she added, "Sis, I know all of this is a lot to take in right now."

"It's crazy, all right."

"And scary," Miranda added. "But trust me, Rayne would never hurt you."

But she wasn't afraid of him. Rather, she was more afraid of herself. Of the feelings warring inside her.

Not because she'd done the unthinkable and fallen in love with him again. Truthfully, she'd never stopped loving him in the first place.

She loved him and he was leaving and it was the past repeating itself all over again.

All the more reason for her to ignore what Miranda was saying, bury herself back under the covers and forget everything. It wasn't as if he could stick around and give her the happily-ever-after she so desperately wanted.

At the same time, Cody was a vampire and it didn't seem to be putting a crimp in his relationship with Miranda. Lucy watched as he slid a possessive arm around her sister and pulled her close. He nuzzled her neck and a thought struck.

"You're not—" she started, but Miranda shook her head.

"Not yet, but I plan on letting Cody turn me when the time is right. We've both agreed that we want to be together forever." She smiled. "He's going to turn me on our wedding night. Our final vow to each other. I'll be there for him and he'll be there for me for the rest of eternity."

"You make it sound so simple."

"It is simple. All that really matters is that he loves me and I love him. As long as that's true, we can work out all the details."

But it wasn't as simple for Lucy and Rayne. For one thing, she didn't even know if he loved her. While Cody and Miranda seemed convinced, he'd never actually said the words and so she couldn't be sure.

And even if he did feel the same, it wouldn't be enough to change his mind. He feared himself. His nature. She'd seen the emotion blazing in his eyes the instant before they'd blazed bright red. She had no doubt he would keep running.

Especially if he loved her.

But if she could convince him otherwise…

"Where are you going?" Miranda asked when she scrambled from the bed and handed over Cupid.

Lucy's gaze collided with her sister's as she shoved her feet into a pair of flip-flops and reached for her car keys. "To fight."

RAYNE TOUCHED HIS Gram's apron that hung on a peg inside the barn door for the last time. He fought against the urge to snatch up the worn fabric and tuck it into his small duffel bag. But he couldn't take the past with him any more than he could change it, and seeing it day after day would just remind him.

He had to let go.

He balled his fingers, snatched up his bag and the signed papers folded in a small envelope, and turned to leave.

That was when he saw Lucy standing in the barn doorway.

His chest tightened and he stiffened. "You shouldn't be here."

"Why?" She arched an eyebrow. "Because you might bite me?"

"That's exactly why."

She shrugged. "Maybe I'm willing to take the risk. Maybe losing a little blood is a small price to pay to keep from losing you." Her gaze collided with his. "I love you." Emotion glittered in the blue depths of her eyes and his heart paused. Pure joy poured through him, followed by a rush of fear—because she didn't know what she was saying.

She didn't know him.

Not now.

He stiffened. "You loved me," he corrected. "A long, long time ago. I loved you, too. But it's different now. I'm different." He forced himself to turn and put a few steps between them when all he really wanted to do was pull her into his arms. "You want a man who'll be around the next day and the day after, and that's not me." He turned to face her. "I'm not a man at all, Lucy. You know that. You saw that. I can't give you a real relationship."

"Why not?"

"Because I'm a vampire, for Chrissake!" He ran a hand over his face as frustration welled inside him. "One minute I'm about to ambush a small group of terrorists in the mountains of Afghanistan and the next thing I know, I've got fangs." He shook his head. "I'm a killer and there isn't a thing I can do about it. If you knew—"

"The past doesn't matter. It doesn't matter what you've done. All that matters is what you do now. You can learn to control it if you want to. If you love me." She stared at him a long moment. "You don't," she stated after a long, silent moment. "That's it, isn't it? I was right in the first place. It was all in my head. You don't feel anything for me. You never did."

"Is that what you really think?" His gaze met hers and he knew she was the one who read his thoughts this time. She saw the emotion blazing and her eyes brightened. Her anxiety eased.

"Love is enough," she told him as she stepped forward. "But you have to give it a chance." She stopped a few inches away from him and stared up into his eyes. "Give us a chance. We can figure all of this out. Cody and Miranda will help. And the others. We can still have a life together."

"The military will be looking for me. I'm AWOL."

"We'll figure something out. Together."

"But what if I hurt you?" he said, voicing the one thought that tormented him. "I wouldn't be able to live with myself."

"You were starving tonight and you didn't so much as scratch me," she pointed out. "And the only way you could really hurt me is by walking away again." Her hand touched his arm and her gaze met his. "I want to be with you, Rayne. From this day forward. For the rest of our lives." When he started to speak, she touched a finger to his lips. "For eternity."

The implication of her words hit him and worry rushed through him. But then she pressed her lips to his and the feeling gave way to an incredible warmth that sank into his bones and erased every doubt. She was right. Love, this love, was the only thing that really mattered. They could figure out the rest.

They would.

Right here in Skull Creek. Together.

"I love you," he spoke the words he should have said so long ago. He slid his arms around her and pulled close.

Epilogue

"ARE YOU SURE you want to do this?" Rayne asked the next night as they stood at the entrance to the Iron Horseshoe.

Lucy glanced at the white ball of fluff in her arms and nodded. "I don't have time for a dog right now. That's why he acts out so much."

"That or he really is possessed by the devil."

Cupid's growl punctuated the statement and Rayne smiled. "I don't think he likes me."

Lucy grinned. "That's a good thing." Her gaze met his. "I was holding on to him for the wrong reasons. I was scared that I would never find someone on my own and he was my insurance policy. But it's time I gave him to someone who can really use him."

She found Becky stacking glasses behind the bar. "What are you doing?" she asked when Lucy handed over Cupid.

"Giving you an edge."

"But what are you going to do?"

"I don't need him anymore." Her gaze caught and held Rayne's and she saw the love she felt for him mirrored in his aqua-blue eyes. "I already found what I'm looking for."

And she didn't intend to let him go.

Never, ever again.

For my readers.

I WISH HE MIGHT...

Samantha Hunter

1

NINA LARSON TRIED TO ignore the slick drip of mud trickling slowly down the middle of her back and pointed a stern finger at the young photographer standing in the corner of the elevator, grinning at her. When he playfully threatened to capture a shot of her, she glared.

"Don't even think about it," she warned.

Sensing imminent harm, he lowered the camera, but couldn't quite get rid of his smirk.

"Well, if it helps, mud looks *really* good on you," he said flirtatiously, letting his gaze drop to her blouse that was also soaked with muddy water, exposing more than she would prefer.

"Hey, eyes up, bucko," was all she said in response as the doors opened.

She ignored the curious gazes as she walked across the maze of cubicles that made up the reporters' bullpen of *The Scoop.* The tabloid was otherwise known as the reporting hell into which she had been relegated after being caught up in a scandal that had cost her being a real reporter at a real newspaper.

Grabbing the door handle of her small office—a cubicle with a ceiling, really—she thanked God for that one small benefit. Upon being hired, she had insisted on her own space, such as it was. She'd taken a pay cut in exchange for this teeny little piece of private real estate, but it was worth it.

She grabbed a raincoat hanging on the back of the door and threw it down on the chair to protect it from her wet, muddy clothes. Sitting at her computer, she wasted no time banging out the copy for her story, due to the copy desk in an hour. There was no time to shower and change until she submitted it, so she set her timer, bore down and got to work.

Her fingers warmed as she typed at lightning speed, the words flying from her fingers as she told the story of Mabel King. The woman, who lived west of the city of Boston in a rural community, claimed that her pig farm boasted mud with special healing qualities, even the ability to reverse the aging process.

Nina titled it Miracles In The Mud? and typed on, flipping through her notes to grab some good quotes and ignoring the part where Mrs. King had dragged her through several yards of deep, sticky, stinky goop between pigs that weren't all too fond of the human intrusion. One disliked it enough to knock Nina backward into the disgusting mud bath.

Nina wasn't feeling any better or any younger for the experience. Still, readers loved a healing mud story, second only to healing properties of hot springs. Some things just never got old. Mabel was thinking about opening a B and B so that she could charge people to roll around in her pig-enhanced mud.

More power to her. In the end, while it was a crock, the modern version of snake oil, it didn't do any harm, either. Everyone did what they had to do to get by in life.

A quick look at the timer told her she had a little time to edit and she did so quickly, finally hitting Send on the internal message system and heaving a sigh of relief.

There. Another amazing tale for *The Scoop* put to bed.

Somehow, it didn't give her the same buzz of satisfaction that writing stories on gang violence or corrupt city politics did. Maybe that was due to the mud drying in the crack of her—

"Nina. Good, you're back," her boss Lindsay said, inviting herself into the office. Lindsay did a once-over, taking in the trail of mud that marked a path to the desk, and then got down to business. "Are you making any progress on the genie story?"

Gee, Lindsay, I'd really like to discuss that after I take a shower, eat and, oh, yeah, throw myself off a bridge, Nina thought sourly. Instead, she shook her head, answering calmly, maintaining what professional demeanor she could. It was all she had left, she figured, and she might as well hang on to it.

"I've done some background research, but—"

"Not good enough. We have to jump on this. You need to find the women on that blog who met that hunk who made wishes come true. Who knows how long genies stick around? Or if this is some kind of scam? Some guy taking advantage of vulnerable women? Either way, there's a story here. I want pictures with this guy, and an interview. Exclusive. This could be your cover, Nina. Don't blow it."

Lindsay was gone before Nina could respond, out to harass another poor soul about their research into space aliens, dogs that dialed 911 to save their owners or seventy-pound babies.

Nina closed her eyes and swallowed hard. She was a professional, a Newhouse-trained journalist who had worked with some of the best and the brightest in the business. She was a professional who got the job done, no matter what the job was.

This was temporary, she reminded herself for the one millionth time. What mattered was that she was working, staying active in her profession and eventually, things would be better. Right?

Right. That was why none of her freelance work had been accepted recently. No one in the business would be forgetting her name for a long time. They wouldn't let her forget what had happened, either. After all, her confidential coverage of a whistle-blower's comments about a company poisoning its employees as it took environmental shortcuts to save money had evaporated when the informant's identity had somehow appeared in the paper. Adding insult to injury, the offenses of the company in question had been drowned out by the scandal.

The man was harassed to the point where he had to sell his house and leave town. She was fortunate that he couldn't come after her legally, but she'd been protected by the paper at the time.

Nina had never used his name and didn't know who included it, or who even knew who her source was, but regardless, it was her fault. He was her informant. It was her job to protect him, and she hadn't. She had to suffer the consequences for that, and she had.

Unfortunately, so had others. What happened had opened the paper to lawsuits and much negative speculation. Several investigative reporters had been hard-pressed to reassure when their own informants who, upon hearing news of the leak, said they didn't trust journalists anymore. Her snafu had nearly compromised many important investigations.

Nina had been quietly asked to quit her job by the man whom she had been sleeping with, no less. It didn't matter that they were madly in love, business was business. Maybe it wasn't smart getting involved with your editor, but love was love.

Nina had wanted to fight. She was innocent, but she couldn't prove it. Peter knew that, but still, he'd asked her, for the sake of the paper, to go. He'd assured her it would blow over and everything would be fine, eventually. She'd find other work.

She'd left, as he'd asked, fading into the background and eventually finding a job at *The Scoop,* the only paper that would take her. She hadn't counted on fading into the background of Peter's life—he had never said anything about that. She'd only heard from Peter twice in the six months since, and she tried to understand. She'd left him with a huge mess to cope with, whether she was innocent or not.

Blinking tears away, she found herself staring at *The Herald*'s Web site; the job posting to fill her spot was still open. She clicked again and saw Peter's smile fill the screen, her heart aching.

Shutting off the computer, she pushed her chair back and stood up from her desk, dried mud flaking everywhere around her, her jeans hardened and crinkling, scraping against her skin.

"Damn," she cursed, looking at the ring of dirt around where she stood.

Grabbing her purse, her jacket and the file with GENIE scrawled across it from her desk, she sighed, then walked out, oblivious to the active newsroom milling around her. She would shower, she would eat, and then…then she would try to find whatever yahoo was out there calling himself a genie.

"I HAVE PIZZA. And beer," Kaelee cajoled, standing in Nina's doorway holding her offerings.

"I shouldn't. I have work," Nina said, completely lacking conviction as the scent of melted cheese and pepperoni made her mouth water.

"It's eight o'clock at night, and you haven't eaten. Work can wait an hour. By the way, did you go to the spa? Your skin looks fantastic," Kaelee said, closing the door behind them as they walked into the entryway.

Nina grimaced. She hated to admit it, but after a hot shower to get rid of the mud, her skin did look amazing.

"Thanks. Just a new mud treatment," she said absently. "Here, put that down and let me grab some plates."

"What are you up to? Are you heading out on another alien hunt?" Kaelee asked, noticing the stack of books and papers on the sofa.

"Genies."

"Huh?"

"Genies. You know, the kind that lives in a bottle? Granting wishes, flying on magic carpets and all of that," Nina informed her friend, distracted by the food. She was starving.

Kaelee's eyes reflected new levels of astonishment. "Seriously?"

"If I'm lyin' I'm dyin'."

"Wow, that is too cool!"

Nina blinked as she offered Kaelee a plate piled with three slices and grabbed a beer from the six-pack.

"Excuse me?"

Kaelee shrugged and fell into step behind Nina, carrying her own plate.

"Well, compared to reading through technical patent documents all day to prepare for the trial I have coming up, tracking down genies sounds like a blast."

Nina was forced to agree. Though Kaelee was a brilliant lawyer, some of the details of the cases she handled were mind-numbingly dull.

Nina took a bite of her pizza and closed her eyes in bliss, enjoying the food and the company for a few minutes before speaking again.

"Well, though there obviously is no such thing as real genies, it is kind of cool. The history is real enough, starting back in King David's time, though genies are said to have existed from the beginning of time, made from the primordial fire. Stories about them can be traced through the centuries in religion and myths up to the current day."

"Don't forget *I Dream of Jeannie,*" Kaelee reminded.

"Oh, I loved that show when I was a kid. I still watch the reruns."

"Me, too."

"It's true, genies are a huge presence in the popular mindset. *I Dream of Jeannie,* as well as Disney's *Aladdin,* were Americanized version of the jinn, or jinni, which is where we got the word *genie* from," Nina explained between bites, taking Kaelee's quiet as an invitation to continue. "Myths say jinn can take human form, and there are different kinds, evil or benevolent, angels or demons. There are people who believe jinn really exist in the same way people believe angels or demons exist. People in other countries believe they interact with them on a daily basis, that the jinn live lives much like we do. I even read one thing that mentioned one of the first jinn being a vampire, which is something you don't hear much of in vampire fiction."

Kaelee set down her plate, nodding. "Guardian angels, boogeymen, vampires, all of that. It's a powerful idea, spirits either watching over us or creating all the havoc in our lives. Not to mention immortality."

"Except that the jinn have a history mired in slavery, as well. They were Solomon's slaves, building his temple, and they are usually enslaved by a master whom they serve, but also resent. When they grant wishes, the wishes can often be deceitful, as the jinn will interpret things to suit themselves, using literal meanings against the wisher, or that kind of thing."

"Hmm. Genies in Boston. Sounds like the last guy I went out with. You remember, the bartender?"

Nina grinned. "He could have been the genie I'm looking for. Who knows?"

"Except he didn't make any of my wishes come true, if you get my drift," Kaelee said dryly, lifting her brow suggestively.

Nina laughed. It was good to have someone to talk to about all of this. Kaelee had never been anything less than supportive through her entire ordeal at *The Herald.* They'd been best friends since college, and for that, Nina was thankful.

"So what do you have to do?" Kaelee asked.

"I called some women who were tagged on a blog, discussing recent experiences with a jinn. They had wishes granted and were trying to find other women who had the same experience, from what I can tell. Lindsay wants me to interview them, but the real trick will be to find the genie and get an interview with him, too. I'm meeting one of the bloggers tomorrow afternoon, downtown."

"You do lead an exciting life."

"This isn't exciting to me, unfortunately. It's aggravating. A daily reminder of how far I've fallen. I don't know how much longer I can do this. Seriously, Kaelee, it all feels like such a waste when there is real news happening out there, everywhere."

Sympathy infused her friend's expression, and Nina was sorry for giving in to the impulse to whine. She was lucky to have a job at all, really, especially when times were so hard and newspapers around the country were closing down, putting a lot of people out of work for good.

"I know it's not your dream job, but try to enjoy what you can. You're not trapped behind a desk, and your stories, while *creative*," she said with a grin, "they make people happy. My mother used to read *The Scoop* compulsively. I think it helped her take her mind off her own troubles, which, as you know, were too many to count with my dad being like he was."

Nina nodded. Kaelee's childhood hadn't been a happy one. Escapism was all fine and good. She did get nice e-mails from readers, and several people had loved her story on porn stars who were trying to fit into suburban neighborhoods. But it wasn't enough for her. It wasn't what she had counted on doing with her life. Still, she quietly declared her whining session over.

"I suppose. Thanks," she said, reaching over to squeeze Kaelee's hand. "You're right. It's work. It pays the rent, and I more or less get to come and go as I please, so what the hell, right? I might get to meet a real genie. Who knows?"

"You never can tell," Kaelee said with a wink and tipped her beer toward Nina in salute. "If he offers you a wish, what would it be?"

"Easy," Nina replied without hesitation, the ache in her chest returning with renewed intensity.

"Aw, hon, you have to let him go," Kaelee urged. "Some new guy, a better guy, might be able to make your wishes come true, and stand by you in the process. Unlike Peter."

"You don't know, Kaelee, it was a difficult situation. He has a lot of responsibilities—"

Kaelee shook her head resolutely. "If he loved you, that was his only responsibility. He should have stood by you, defended you, and he didn't. I don't know why you can't see that. Get angry, but don't be sad over a jerk like Peter Wiley."

Nina bit down on her defensive reply. Kaelee had boyfriends aplenty, men were lined up at her door, though because of her parents' disaster of a marriage, Kaelee had declared herself a confirmed single, period. It made it easy with her job, which was the love of her life.

Nina was never short of invitations from men, either, but she had really imagined having it all—the job, the husband, the family. But she'd also had a harder time meeting men who didn't mind the demands of being an investigative reporter. Now it was even worse. Before, they had just balked at her commitment to her job and the dangerous situations she found herself in. Now, the minute her date found out that she worked for *The Scoop,* they thought she was a joke.

Peter hadn't just been her lover. They'd shared the same love of the paper, of the news. He understood when she couldn't be available for a date because she was eyeball deep in a story, or when she met informants in questionable places late at night. He wanted all the same things she did.

"I know it's hard for you to understand, but when you love someone, it's not that easy to leave it all behind," Nina tried to explain, though she knew Kaelee wouldn't get it. She wasn't interested in love. Nina was, and she knew what it was like—and now she knew what it was like to lose it, as well.

Kaelee looked as if she had more to say, but didn't. The two friends finished their meal in silence, yet for the rest of the night Nina couldn't help but fantasize about wishes and the magic creatures who could grant them. If only they really did exist.

2

NINA WATCHED THE WOMAN across from her polish off her second burrito—the price of an interview—and took notes over her own dinner, turning cold on the plate.

"So, your wishes actually came true?" Nina asked neutrally, relying on her reporter training to hide her skepticism. It was clear this woman actually believed she had met a jinn.

"Yes, and then some," the svelte redhead answered, sitting back to grab her bag and ignoring Nina while she dug something out of the bottom. "Listen, I know it sounds crazy, but here, look at this. You can use it if you want," Zoe Mitchell offered with enthusiasm.

Nina had to admit the legal secretary didn't seem like a kook, but her story of meeting the genie was obviously a joke and Nina was waiting for the punch line.

"That was me, a month ago," Zoe announced proudly.

Nina took in the picture showing a grossly overweight version of the woman sitting across from her, and then looked up again.

"No way. Did you have that stomach-stapling surgery or something?"

"No. For one thing, I couldn't have lost this much weight in a month, even with that, and besides, do you see one loose bit of skin anywhere?"

Nina had to admit, Zoe was the definition of a hard ody. She shook her head in response to the question. laybe the photo was older than Zoe was admitting to, iough Zoe had been clever, holding up a newspaper with ie date in her photo—could it had been a mock-up? Nina iade a note to check the newspaper headlines for that ate and compare them.

"My last wish was to be skinny and sexy, to have the erfect body, but I still wanted to be able to eat as much as want of anything I want. The next day, I woke up and oilà!" she said, gesturing to a body that didn't look like it ould handle two giant burritos in a row, though it just had.

Nina thought this has to be a hook to lure the unsus-ecting into a weight-loss scam of some sort. Zoe would robably head for the nearest ladies' room to purge those urritos as soon as no one was looking. If she could uncover he scam, that was her story, which made her feel mar-inally better. Otherwise, she would be writing fiction about woman who got three wishes granted. So, the most logical vay to pressure this woman into hopefully exposing her cam was to play along and to make her provide more proof han a trumped-up picture if she wanted Nina to believe here were really genies at work. She wouldn't be able to lo that, which would be the first step in exposing the scam.

Settling back in, Nina nodded. "Okay, using the picture vould be great, thanks. But for a cover story, I need more roof. I would need others, maybe people at your workplace, o attest that you lost this weight seemingly overnight. Most f all, I need an interview with the man himself, the genie."

"Well, that's not going to be possible," Zoe said, her ace falling.

"Why not?"

"He, Alec, said that other people don't realize there's been a change. They just see you as you are."

Convenient, Nina thought, but kept a straight face.

"Okay, so where is he? Alec?"

"I don't know where he is anymore. After my wish, he just disappeared, and so did the ring."

"The ring you found while you were swimming?"

Nina looked at her notes. Zoe said she had been doing laps in the community pool when onlookers shouted cruel things about her size. It had been one of the worst moments of her adult life, because though she enjoyed the exercise, she knew she couldn't keep swimming and exposing herself to ridicule. Everything seemed hopeless, as she had tried diet after diet, with no success.

When she started to swim toward the ladder to exit the pool, she looked down and saw a gold ring at the bottom. She said she'd felt called by it, and swam down to retrieve it, even though she didn't like going far underwater.

The next thing she knew, she was standing in front of a hottie in the locker room who was making wishes come true.

"Yes."

"But you have no idea where he is now?"

"Nope. We've been trying to track him through the blog, hoping people would see and check in, but it's been impossible to tell who's jerking us around or not. Some people post that they have seen a genie, too, but they really haven't," she said, shrugging. "He just shows up when he wants to, I guess."

"Did he ever try anything funny? Asking for money, sex or anything else?"

"No, nothing. He said he was there to grant my three wishes, and that's all he did. But he did seem…I don't know, kind of distant, and maybe even a little sad. He didn't say much, to be honest. Hard to believe a guy that hot could be lonely, but you know, he never laid a hand on me. If I'd had a fourth wish, maybe…but as it is, I'm not having any trouble with men now," Zoe said with a grin.

"I bet. And how do you think he picked you?" Nina asked.

"I have no idea, I'm just glad he did. It changed my life forever. I go on dates, I feel wonderful. I have sex. I have a *life*. You can believe it or not, but it's real."

With a nod, Nina shut off the tape recorder that sat on the table between them, knowing the last bit was very quotable, so at least that was something. She had Zoe sign the release form for the article and offered to mail the picture back once she was done with it. The woman waved her off.

"I never want to see that picture again. This is the new me, and I'd rather forget the past," Zoe said with conviction, saying a quick goodbye and leaving as Nina paid the bill.

Doubts followed her out the door. Zoe seemed so normal, so sincere, but then the best con artists were very convincing, weren't they? Still, Zoe hadn't tried to sell her anything but the story, hadn't tried to string her along for more.

Could the young woman be ill? Could that explain her sudden weight loss and her illusions of a handsome man who changed her life?

There had to be some rational explanation.

Nina stopped in her tracks by the edge of an alley where she heard a muffled noise. It was late May, and late in the afternoon the sun lay low. The alley was dim. Peering between the buildings, she tried to see if there was trouble, her phone in her hand in case she had to call 911.

The shuffling sound came again and she stepped forward carefully, hugging the brick wall behind her and trying to focus in the faint light. Her years as a reporter had taken her to worse spots. If someone was in trouble, she felt the need to find out and to help.

The noise got louder, and Nina jumped out of her skin as a small gray cat ran by her legs, scooting down the length of the alley and out to the street. Calming her heartbeat, she turned to leave, her eye catching something by her foot, glimmering in the low light.

A ring.

"Oh, come on," she said, the sardonic comment echoing in the alley.

Bending down, she used her key to pluck the gold ring from between the cracks of the pavement, rubbing the dirt away and checking it out. She was no expert, but it was heavy and solid, probably real gold, and it looked as if it had been stuck in the ground for a while. Maybe stolen from some poor guy who'd been mugged on the street, or lost by someone having an assignation in the alley. No way could it be the same ring.

Slipping it in her pocket, Nina headed back out to the street and toward the T-Station, her fingers absently caressing the smooth band of gold all the way home.

LATER THAT NIGHT, Nina tried to work. But she'd been sitting at her laptop before the empty page for hours, completely unmotivated. Somehow she hadn't pulled what she had on the genie story so far into any kind of coherent unit.

She had no evidence of anything. Just some research, a picture and a few usable quotes. She needed much more.

The idea that she might lose this job for lack of being able to get an exclusive interview with a genie was absurd. Lindsay hadn't threatened her with her job, not exactly, but her most recent e-mail regarding the story's progress wasn't encouraging. If she lost her position at *The Scoop,* there wasn't anywhere left to go.

Standing and pacing for a few minutes in frustration, Nina stalked across the room and poured a glass of wine, proceeding to do exactly what she knew she shouldn't do.

Reaching down to open a drawer under one of her side tables, she retrieved some old pictures that she and Peter had taken on their one trip together. Carrying the wine and the pictures back to her room, she plopped down among the pillows on her bed to try to remember what it was like to be very, truly happy. Satisfied with life, full of hope for the future, without a doubt it would all happen.

Now, there was nothing but doubt.

She'd sent Peter an e-mail when she got home, but there had been no response. She knew he was online, having seen him commenting over on Twitter, and yet he ignored her. Could Kaelee be right? Was she just being a romantic fool?

Her eyes blurred and burnt and she angrily wiped away tears.

"Dammit, I *do* have to stop this," she said angrily to herself, wishing away the wave of self-pity, but finding it creeping up on her anyway.

Kaelee *was* right. Peter didn't care about her anymore, and maybe he never really had, but what about how she felt? How was she supposed to stop loving him and mourning what she had lost?

Her eye landed upon the gold ring sitting on the bedside table and she reached for it, playing it between her fingers. It was a gorgeous ring, a symbol of everlasting commitment, but someone had lost it in an alley. Nina had put a classified online but sincerely doubted it would find its rightful owner.

She wondered about the person who'd lost it, if he had really loved anyone. If he was saddened by the loss, or had been happy to leave it lying in the dirt.

She finally gave in, realizing the phone wasn't going to ring. Peter wasn't going to answer her e-mail, and she had no story to hand in to Lindsay tomorrow. Sliding the ring on her finger, even though it was too large, she gave in to tears until she fell mercifully asleep.

Only to be shocked awake what felt like seconds—though the clock said hours—later.

Someone sat at the side of her bed. As she opened her mouth to scream, her mind racing to think of where she'd left her cell phone, he spoke in a calming tone.

"Don't be afraid, I mean no harm. I'm the jinn you seek. I'm here to make your wishes come true."

ALEC WATCHED THE LOVELY woman with riotous black curls framing a heart-shaped face that had turned pale upon discovering him sitting at her bedside. Sleep-laden brown eyes went wide as she drew back against the headboard, her full breasts pushing against the fabric of her pajamas as she strained to put some distance between them. The fabric was thick and practical, pants and a shirt that covered everything, and yet the simple impression of her nipples budding against the inside of the material stirred him.

As he looked at this woman, it was as if a thousand flames danced over his skin. He hadn't experienced true desire in a very long time; the sudden spark took him somewhat by surprise. He moved to the side of the bed, leaning in closer.

"You sought me, did you not? You wear my ring."

While watching her sleep, he'd slipped into her dreams, met her there and asked her what made her so sad, not that he needed to ask. When a jinn walked in someone's dreams, he touched a part of their soul, saw their secrets.

What he saw in Nina's dreams made him feel things he didn't often allow himself to feel. What was the point? As a jinn, a fire spirit who only existed to serve the needs and wishes of others, he and his kind were not meant for love.

Alec looked at Nina deeply, sliding to the side of the bed, watching her fear turn to curiosity, the knot of her fingers relaxing slightly where she clutched the blanket. He would be familiar to her, though she wouldn't know exactly why. She wouldn't remember—

"You're from my dream," she said suddenly, shocking his thoughts into silence and he watched understanding enter her eyes. "I'm still dreaming. Of course," she said with no small measure of relief. "You're Alec."

She wasn't dreaming, of course, but that she remembered him specifically was disturbing. Jinn were never seen, never remembered, unless they wanted to be.

"You're not dreaming," he said, laying his palm along the top of her thigh, sliding it upward. "Should I show you how real I am?"

She drew her leg away quickly. "Hey, stop that. This isn't *that* kind of dream."

"What if I changed how I look? Would you believe me then?"

With merely a thought, he remembered the image of the other man in her dreams, the one she longed for, and became him. Her lips parted as she watched him, her breath coming a little faster.

"Peter?" she whispered, and reached out her hand to touch his face.

Alec shuddered, the softness of the touch making him hard and needy within seconds. He was a spirit, but he took the presence of a real man—or any other shape he desired—and was able to feel, act and react like any other human. Right now, that fact tortured him as he ached to take the woman in front of him. *It would be easy enough,* he thought. She thought she was in a dream, and he knew a thousand ways to please her....

"I can be whoever you want me to be," he said, leaning in, slipping his hand up underneath the soft fabric to caress the soft skin of her belly as he focused on her lips. Her tongue darted out, hungry for him, but right before he took her lips, she pushed him back.

"No. You aren't Peter. You aren't *real,*" she said, her tone laced with pain.

"If I am only a dream, then what is the harm? You can give in," he cajoled, unsure why he was so intent on seducing her, but finding himself compelled to do so. Maybe he had simply denied himself for too long. If not this woman, it might have been any other.

He focused magic through his touch, his fingers still

splayed across her stomach, moving slowly toward the softer flesh that formed the delectable peak under her nightshirt. She wouldn't be able to resist him, especially in this form.

"*What's the harm?*" she practically hissed back at him, pushing him away before his hand closed over her breast and scuttling to the other side of the bed. She stood, tall for a woman but still only coming to his shoulder. There was no mistaking her stormy glare.

"The harm is that if I remember what it's like to be with him, and then I wake up a-alone," she said haltingly, biting her lip and holding back tears that he could see shimmering in the low, warm light of the room. "I can't take that."

Her arms fell from their defensive position at her front to her sides as she slumped back down to sit on the other side of the bed. "I want to wake up now," she said dispiritedly, closing her eyes hard.

He waited while she did whatever it was she was doing. She opened her eyes again and turned in his direction.

"You're still here."

"Yes." he said, turning back to himself. "I told you, this is not a dream. I am jinn. You found the ring and by slipping it on your finger, your tears touching it, you released me from its bondage. Now I am yours to command."

It wasn't strictly true, Alec knew. He was bound to honor her three wishes, though he could do so in any interpretation of them that he wished—a magical loophole—but he didn't have to do anything else she said. For some reason, though, he didn't mind the idea of being her slave—or maybe having her be his.

"Fine. If you say so. I'd like to command an interview, first of all. I need one for my paper."

A smile pulled at the corner of his lips. She was petulant, playing along, still believing she was caught in some strange dream. She also hadn't wished for the interview, so he could sidestep that one for now.

"Of all the things you could wish for, you would wish for that? To ask me questions?"

"No, it's not a wish, it's a command."

The grin broke loose and he laughed. Most wanted wealth, beauty, revenge, his body or someone else's, immediately. This luscious woman, who believed he was only a dream, wanted an interview for her newspaper.

"Fine. What if I promise you an interview—later?"

"When?"

"After I grant your wishes. The interview I will do because I want to."

"Really?"

"Yes. So you can, uh, confirm your source?" he said, grasping for the language she would understand. "Make sure I am who I say I am."

This time she laughed. Her face lit up when she laughed, and he thought it one of the most beautiful sights he had ever seen. Over a thousand years, Alec had seen a lot.

"I guess that's true. I wouldn't expect a genie to be so concerned about research, but since you are just a figment of my imagination to begin with, I guess it makes sense."

"Do you need time to think about your wish?"

The sadness replaced her smile again, and he almost wished he hadn't reminded her. He knew what she was going to wish for and while part of him wanted to tell her how foolish it was, that was not his place. Most humans wished for stupid, vain things.

"I can wish for anything?"

"Almost. You cannot wish for immortality, more wishes or to make someone return from the dead."

Her pretty nose wrinkled. "Ick, no, I don't want that. I just want the man I love back in my life."

"He is not dead?" Alec asked, pretending ignorance.

"No, of course not. We just had a…falling-out that's keeping us apart. It's not his fault. It's…complicated."

"So all you wish is that he would want to be with you?" Alec led her along, rephrasing the wish to his liking, another jinn trick.

"Yes. Yes, please. I always wonder if he has missed me as much as I miss him. I wish we could be together, just like it was before," she said with a sincere longing so full of ache that it made Alec's chest tighten. This woman chased her own unhappiness, but it was not for him to judge.

"Granted."

"Just like that?"

"Yes. Sleep, Nina, and in the morning, you will find your wish has come to pass."

He watched her eyelids become heavy, a small smile lifting the corner of her generous mouth as she lay back down on the pillows.

"I don't believe you," she murmured before falling back to a deep sleep.

Alec leaned down, unable to resist one brief taste of her lips, and whispered against them, "You will."

3

NINA PULLED ON a yellow cashmere sweater that her mother had sent her for her birthday. At the paper, she'd always worn less colorful, more unisex clothes appropriate for the job. Now, there was no reason not to indulge her love for bright color. One perk of her *Scoop* job was that they didn't care what she wore as long as stories were handed in on time. Personality and eccentricity was almost rewarded there, which Nina grudgingly admitted was a welcome perk. She had tired of gray suits.

It was nice of her dream jinn to offer her an interview, but she had more leads to chase down if she was going to get this story in at all. Maybe the other women on the blog would be able to give her more leads than Zoe. Pausing in front of her bed, she swore she could feel the dream jinn's hand on her skin, the force of the dream revisited. It certainly had seemed real enough.

He'd been so imposing, a big man, tall and muscular, his copper skin gleaming under an ivory satin vest that stoked her imagination. Dark, flowing pants that hid powerful legs, and other delectable surprises. His hands had been gentle, his touch warm, seductive against her skin.

Before he had appeared to her as Peter, she'd been

unable to look away from his mesmerizing gray eyes, thickly lashed. His jet-black hair was long, pulled back tightly, away from his face, accenting regal features, his lips sensual and full for a man.

She'd always preferred the cooler, businesslike appearance of patrician, Anglo men such as Peter. Her former lover wasn't muscular or macho, but wore his suits with a urbane kind of grace. Muscles and seductive eyes had never been her weakness—until now, it seemed.

Shaking her head, she smiled at her own musings. Her imagination had just cooked up some version of what she had been reading about, that was all: dark, exotic men who made women's wishes come true.

Right.

Stuffing all of her research in her bag, she grabbed her BlackBerry and started to do a quick e-mail check as she ran out the door, and what she saw stopped her in her tracks.

Sweetheart, woke up this morning missing you. Must see you today. Meet me at noon? Peter.

She blinked and reloaded the message a few times to make sure that her eyes weren't playing tricks on her, but it was always still there.

Peter did love her, and he wanted to see her. He was *dying* without her. She read the words again, doing a little happy dance by the door, her entire body absolutely vibrating with excitement. It was almost ten now. She had to change; no way could she meet Peter in these casual clothes.

Popping off a short e-mail, she told Lindsay that she had interviews and wouldn't be into the office for most of the day. What did it matter anyway? Maybe this was the first step in her getting her old life back. Once she and Peter were together again, she was sure he could pull some strings for her. Maybe he'd just been waiting, letting it all fall behind them, getting some distance from that mess so that now they could move forward.

She might not get rehired at *The Herald*, but it was possible her *Scoop* days were over.

Bouncing back to her bedroom she sent him an enthusiastic YES.

How to prepare to see the man you loved after a six-month separation? She knew what she hoped would happen, and that meant pulling out the sexiest underwear she had and ditching the sweater and pants. When she saw Peter, she wanted to look like the woman he'd fallen in love with.

As she changed into different outfits, primping and fantasizing about the afternoon meeting, her thoughts landed on the memory of her jinn dream, the handsome genie promising her that her dream would come true.

A shiver worked its way down her spine as his face seemed to appear in front of her eyes again, those seductive dark eyes watching her as she took in the sleek red lace, push-up bra and sheer stockings complete with garters. *Crazy*, she thought, shaking her head to clear it. Pulling on a conservative gray skirt and jacket over it, she started to feel like her old self.

This would drive Peter wild, she thought with a smile, turning her attention to jewelry and perfume. Silently, however, she thanked the universe, her imaginary jinn, Alec, or whoever it was that made wishes come true.

ALEC WATCHED AS NINA rushed back into her bedroom, her cheeks flushed, her dark eyes shining with excitement. She couldn't see him sitting in the corner. For now, it was better she thought he was the stuff of dreams.

He turned away, summoning the energy to leave her in privacy, though that was difficult; his curiosity to see her without clothing was intense. Instead, he would leave and find another of his kind until she called for him again. The thought had a particular sourness as he watched her get ready to meet her lover. He pushed the thoughts away.

Jealousy was something he'd left behind centuries ago, along with many other useless emotions. He belonged to no one, and no one had ever belonged to him. Jealousy was for humans, who only held their possessions for such a short time. It served no purpose for an immortal.

"You look troubled, Alec," the familiar voice of his friend, known among the jinn as Ahja, spoke as Alec found himself standing before a long, teak bar, shining glasses hanging overhead, the bottles stacked neatly behind. He smiled at Ahja, who wore the name tag Joe.

"Joe, huh?"

"Yes. As in 'regular Joe.' That's me."

"Right. Since when do you take on human work, Joe?"

His friend smiled wickedly, and Alec followed Joe's glance to where a young, nubile waitress took an order from two men sitting at a table, watching a baseball game.

"Since her," Joe clarified.

"Your current mistress?"

The bartender poured Alec a whiskey and leaned in to say in a low voice, "In every sense of the word."

Alec shook his head. Joe loved women, and he was

also a very, very old jinn. Far older than Alec, though right now he looked like any other human male in his thirties.

"She finds that she likes a man of experience. Tired of boys," Ahja said with confidence gleaned over millennia. "She has yet to make her first wish, so I think we'll have quite a bit of fun together before she does so."

Many jinn didn't reveal their true nature to their holders—the name of the one who held their vessel, the object to which they had been attached. Delaying wishes was a way of staying in human form for long periods of time, enjoying life as much as possible. Jinn could live as human, though they were not. When it was possible to be trapped inside a ring, bottle or a lamp for hundreds of years, they had become very creative about finding ways to stretch their time outside.

The risk was when the holder figured out the same trick and would enslave the jinn to other kinds of service, spacing out wishes by years and decades in order to keep him. Jinn, for all of their power, were slaves to one of the lowest races—humans. While there were dangers, most of their associations were mundane or pleasant, however. It made Alec think of Nina again. He wondered if she was in Peter's bed at this very moment.

"I imagine you will teach her well," Alec said, taking a sip of the whiskey and enjoying the way the spicy liquid warmed him. Jinn all loved anything made of fire, as they were, including good liquor. He could never get drunk, so it wasn't a problem.

"So, as to your troubles?" Joe inquired, washing out a glass with a white cloth.

"No troubles," Alec denied, but Joe was too perceptive.

"Hey, man, I'm a bartender. Spill it."

Alec had to grin, but shook his head. "You know the drill. My mistress is a nice woman, but she loves a jerk and wants him anyway. Her first wish was to get him back in her life." Alec took another drink and set the glass down. "She's going to get her wish, and I fear she is not going to like it."

Joe set the glass down, shrugging. "So? That's what we do. And at least you are doing her a favor, showing her the truth."

"She won't see it that way, I imagine."

"Who cares?" Joe's eyes widened, and he whistled low into the air between them. "You like her. You *care*."

"I wouldn't say that, exactly," Alec denied, but could hear the lie in his own voice.

"Alec, you know better than to let your emotions get involved in jinn business," Joe said, his own eyes cold and hard. "It can only lead to pain. It's better to play and deceive, to have fun," he said with a meaningful glance toward the cute waitress who blew him a kiss. "But that's all."

"I know," Alec agreed. "I'll get the wishes done and move on."

"Good. There are murmurings among the others. We're being tracked."

Alec nodded. "I think I know of what they speak. The woman I am with now, she's a reporter—nothing serious, one of the tabloids—but she was researching jinn, and spoke with my former holder. It seems harmless. She doesn't even believe I am real."

Joe nodded shortly, leaning forward with his elbows on

the edge of the bar. "Be careful. You don't know what her tricks are, and you can never trust them."

"Humans, yes."

"Especially women. I heard of something much more dangerous than a reporter, someone setting a trap. Be careful, my friend," Joe warned.

Alec was sure whoever was trying to trap a jinn—and people who believed did it all the time, seeking a quick route to wealth or power—that it wasn't Nina Larson.

"I'll be careful," he promised and meant it, because getting too close was dangerous, if not for the reasons Joe thought. It was because when Nina released him, sending him back to the ring, which was inevitable, she would move on, and he would be left to suffer the consequences for eternity.

COPLEY SQUARE WAS bursting with people worshipping spring, eating lunch on the steps of the Boston Public Library and reading on benches while others milled around the offerings of the Farmers' Market. Nina barely saw any of them as she walked quickly across the square toward the Schön sculpture of the Tortoise and Hare where she and Peter had first kissed. They always knew to meet each other there without needing to say so. The sculpture commemorated the runners of the Boston Marathon, fast and slow alike, and Peter loved it because he ran the race each year. Nina, who had never run anywhere except after a story, preferred to be the hare.

Her heart beat a little faster as she saw his familiar profile as he stood waiting, wearing his business suit as nicely as ever, his ear pasted to his cell phone as usual. She smiled, flexing her fingers in anticipation of touching him again. Finally.

"Peter," she said from behind, smiling as he spun to face her, his eyes bright with pleasure as he cut the call short and smiled broadly.

"Nina, sweetheart," he said warmly.

She stepped in for an embrace. "It's so good to see you, Peter. I've missed you terribly," she confessed, looking up into his face, focusing on his mouth, badly wanting the kiss that his eyes were promising.

"I've been dying to see you, too, love," he said, but he didn't kiss her. Instead, he stepped back with a smile. "I have a private lunch arranged at the Westin," he added, the heat flaring in his eyes.

Nina paused, momentarily disconcerted by the cool welcome, and the way he stepped away from her touch.

"Lunch at a hotel? Why not the usual spot?"

"I wanted to be alone with you. We have a lot to...catch up on," he said in a tone that told her conversation wasn't all he was thinking about. "I reserved a suite and ordered us lunch there. Come with me, Nina. I've been hardly able to think straight for wanting to be alone with you," he said, not bothering to disguise the desire in his voice.

Though something felt off, she smiled and fell into step beside him as they crossed the square. How could she resist his plea? Of course it made sense that he wanted them to be alone, not sitting in the middle of a crowded café full of power brokers.

"That was sweet of you, Peter, to book a room." She looked down, taking a breath. "I wondered why you haven't answered my e-mails, though, or my phone calls?"

He put his hand at the small of her back as they crossed the busy street heading toward the hotel. "I was just busy, darling. It's been a madhouse without you, and it's been hell trying to undo some of the damage at the paper," he said absently, watching traffic.

"What about the damage to me?" she asked, moving away from his hand as they walked toward the hotel entrance.

He turned toward her, his gaze contrite. "I know, I know. It's haunted me, not being able to be there for you. I hate the thought of you working at that...*rag*. Hate that you ever had to leave," he said miserably enough to console her as they walked inside, but Kaelee's voice asking her *why* he hadn't stood by her buzzed around her mind like an annoying bug. She ignored it.

"I know. I hated it, too, every day. I thought I had lost everything, including you," she replied. As the elevator doors closed, conversation was cut off as he pulled her up against him and covered her mouth in a scorching kiss.

Maybe it was the chill of the intervening months, or that so much still had to be said between them, but for some reason, Peter's kiss wasn't curling her toes like it used to do. She tried to relax and wrapped her arms around his neck, earning a groan of approval as he pushed her back against the wall of the elevator, the hard ridge under his slacks pressing into her belly.

"Peter, wait, not here," she said breathlessly, breaking the kiss as his hand found its way under her skirt.

He turned, hit the buttons that would stop the car between floors and faced her with a wicked smile. Hunger penetrated every nuance of his features. She felt more like a snack than the woman he loved.

"Why not? We've been apart so long. I want you so much. It's all I can think about, getting inside you right here, right now," he said, leaning in for another kiss, but Nina felt herself tense up instead of responding to his passion.

He was confused, too, and frustrated.

"What's wrong, Nina?"

"I don't know. There's just so much to talk about. And we've barely spoken for months, and I thought you'd want to, I don't know…reconnect, I guess," she said weakly.

"Nina, I want you so much I can't think straight. We'll have time to talk later. We'll have all the time in the world…"

Relief warmed her and she smiled, closing her eyes and blowing out a breath as she relaxed against him. "Oh, Peter, *that's* what I needed to hear, that we're going to have a future together. I'm sorry I froze up. I guess I just needed to hear that you love me, and you want me in your life on a regular basis again," she said, but now Peter had a very strange look on his face.

She lifted a hand, touching him. "Peter? Is everything okay?"

He kissed the palm of her hand, nipping lightly as he pulled her in closer.

"Everything is fine, Nina. But you do understand, well…we never made any promises. I want you in my life, but…things are more complicated now."

"What do you mean?"

He buried his head in her neck, kissing her in a sensitive spot that made her thoughts blur for a moment, his voice muffled as he said, "We can't be a couple, not out in the open, like we were, but we can have this. The heat, the passion…I can't imagine ever wanting anyone as much as I want you."

Nina's heart fell, and she pushed away. "Peter, you have been telling me how much you want me, but what about how much you *love* me?"

"Well, of course I care for you, but—"

He *cared* for her?

"But what? There is no but! You either love me and want a life with me, putting the past behind us, or you don't."

"It doesn't have to be an either-or, Nina. You were always like that, drawing lines in the sand," he said with a degree of irritation. "But you have to admit, we were always best in bed, anyway."

Her insides might as well have hardened to ice at his words. She was so frozen in place that he took her silence for acquiescence and smiled.

"We can have a very good time together, Nina, like we always did."

Without a word, she turned to hit the down button on the elevator panel.

"Peter, tell me one thing."

"What? Why did you press Down?"

"Did you plan to contact me at all before today?"

His brow wrinkled and he shook his head. "I don't know where you're going with this."

"When did you come up with the idea of us being no-strings sex buddies?"

"Well, I have to admit, after you left the paper, I hadn't figured we'd see each other again, but then I woke up this morning missing you. It was the strangest thing, but I realized no woman had ever satisfied me as much as you did. I knew we had to get back together, even though I'm taking a chance with my reputation, and—"

She held up her hand as the doors opened. She wasn't sure if her heart was breaking or if it was just sheer humiliation that gripped her, but she kept it together enough to sound cool and collected. "I understand, Peter, and you can just keep on wanting. Goodbye, Peter. Don't contact me again."

4

ALEC VISITED NINA again later that night, but only stood watching her sleep, doing nothing but taking her in. Her suit was thrown over a chair, and she was stretched out in the gorgeous red lace she'd worn under it.

For him.

Alec was relieved to find her alone, but checked the emotion.

"*You.* You tricked me," Nina accused him, her eyes flying open and pinning him.

He sighed heavily. No doubt she would think she was dreaming again. Her cheeks were flushed with anger, her eyes flashing. Pert breasts pushed against the red lace of the lingerie she wore—very different from the flannel of the previous night—and he let his eyes linger before he answered.

"I granted your wish. You said you wished you could be with him like you were before. That happened, did it not?"

"No! You know very well what happened," she snapped, choking out the words as tears filled her eyes. Alec wanted to believe he was not affected by her pain, but he'd be lying to himself.

"He only wanted me for *sex*. He said we could never be together, not openly. He said he was taking chances with his reputation by being with me," she said. "But that's what *you* made happen, isn't it? You made him act that way toward me. You took my wish and you twisted it to make it something that wasn't real."

"I did take your wish literally," he admitted. "But even I can't change the love that is—or isn't—in someone's heart. If he loved you, nothing would be able to interfere with that. You asked for things to be like they were before. It's exactly how he felt about you before, but he lied about it then."

"No, he loved me. I know he did."

"How can you know? He said this?" Alec asked, knowing full well the answer from the look on her face. It was probably only just dawning on Nina that if there had been any love in her previous arrangement, she was the only one who had felt it. Probably Peter had lied only to get her into bed.

Alec said gently, "It sounds like you are well rid of the *orospu çocuğu*," he added.

Nina sniffed, wiping at her eyes. Alec couldn't keep himself from watching the sway of her breasts as she moved. "Oros…what?"

"Uh, roughly, in my native tongue, a bastard," he explained with a slight smile.

"Which is?" Nina asked, seeming momentarily distracted from her problems.

"I speak many languages, some you would have never heard of, but the language of my youth is an early form of Turkish. I was born in an area known as Mesopotamia," he explained, moving to sit closer, tracing his fingertips over her cheek where her tears still felt wet. He couldn't help it. In spite of Joe's warnings, he had to touch Nina.

"And your name is Alec? That's very modern," she said doubtfully.

"I have had many names. Jinn never reveal their true name. It gives the owner too much power to enslave them," he said very seriously. "Alec fits, for now."

"So how old are you?"

Alec's eyes narrowed. "Are you interviewing me?" he asked with a slight edge of incredulity.

She shrugged. "I figured I needed to get something useful from this mess. It's clear things with Peter are over, and I can't afford to lose my job."

"I can grant you wealth, power, anything you want," Alec said, his eyes meeting hers. "Just ask."

Nina sighed. "I've never cared if I was wealthy. I only want to do the thing I was meant to do. I enjoy my work, or I used to."

"All you have to do is wish."

She looked at him skeptically. Even so, he was happy to see that at least her tears had vanished.

"First of all, you are just a dream, and second of all, I like to take credit for my own accomplishments. I never ask for anything to be handed to me and I'm not starting now," she said stubbornly.

Alec smiled. "Then, maybe you should make a wish of a more...intimate nature," he suggested in a low tone, feeling his body harden, wanting to push her onto the soft pillows and explore every inch of what was under the red lace.

"Oh...I don't know," she said uncertainly, but sighed

when he pressed a kiss to her throat. "Then again, this is just a dream. Why not?"

"Indeed," he said, watching the pink pearls of her nipples bud underneath the bra, and the blush that overcame her take on a different tone, heat rising between them.

He wanted her. He could make her his, make her inadvertently spend her wishes on the many pleasures he would bring her, and then he would move on to his next master. She would only remember him as a dream. It was better this way, given the emotions she made him feel. The sooner he was away from her, the better.

He would take her to the edge, make her wish and then make her beg.

She was still in the sexy underwear she'd dressed in that morning. Leaning down, he closed his mouth over the lace-covered tip of her breast, satisfied at her uninhibited response.

Slipping his fingers under the thin straps of the bra, he drew them down over her shoulders, peeling back the thin bit of fabric that covered her breasts, and revealed her to his perusal.

"Lovely… You're perfect, you know," he murmured, bending his head to suckle the sweet flesh and enjoying the way she arched beneath him, looking for more. He gave it to her, using his hands to press her breasts together, and sucking the tender tips into his mouth simultaneously until she was writhing and whimpering from his kisses.

When he pulled away and looked down at her, he was satisfied that she wasn't thinking about the man who had rejected her, but only of him. Her breath came in short little panting sounds, her breasts pink where he had suckled her, the nipples rigid and ready for more.

"What do you want, *aşik?* You can wish for anything. I can become any man, or woman, you have ever imagined being with. I can love you in any way you desire. All you have to do is wish…" he tempted, sliding his hands up and down her silky thighs in a mesmerizing rhythm.

"This is a great dream," she said breathlessly, her eyes meeting his, but then her next words undid him completely. "But I don't think I need to wish for anything more than you, Alec."

Alec, shaken to his core by the words, forgot about drawing forth her wishes. He forgot that, to Nina, he was nothing but a figment of her imagination. He couldn't think of anything but touching her everywhere, loving her completely.

He smoothed his palm over her hip, and where it slid over the lace covering her, the material instantly disappeared, leaving her naked to his gaze.

"Oh," she breathed, watching as his hands traveled up, touching every inch, until she was completely naked before him.

He rose by the side of the bed, his eyes not leaving hers as he read her fantasies. And while he could have disposed of his own clothing just as easily, he smiled wickedly and disrobed before her, slowly, offering himself to her hungry eyes bit by tantalizing bit.

When he let his loose satin pants fall to the floor, exposing himself to her view, he enjoyed the way her fingers curled into the sheets, her eyes wide as they moved from his erect phallus to his eyes. He reached down, stroked his hard shaft. Her lips parted, her tongue darting out to wet them.

"If I am not pleasing to you, mistress, I can be what you need. Longer, heavier, harder—"

"You're perfect," she choked out as she swung her legs over the side of the bed and sat before him, bringing them close together. She stopped the movement of his hand with hers, dipping her head down to kiss the head of his cock, drawing a deep groan from him. He started to pull back, but she looked up at him, her eyes turned to onyx pools.

"Don't you like it?"

"Too much, Nina…it's my place to pleasure you."

She smiled at him, and he caught his breath at the open passion in her expression as she slid from the bed to her knees, poised before him. "Then let me take what I want," she said, taking him wholly into the sweet well of her mouth, drawing backward with her lips sealed tightly around him.

Alec's head lolled, his hands burying themselves in her black mane of hair as he gritted his teeth against the need to push deeper to find the satisfaction he had to hold back. He had never lost control, having eons of sexual experience. But when he looked down at her ruby lips wrapped around him, her eyes closed in rapture, the slight vibration of her moans massaging his shaft as she slid forward and back, he had to fight not to give in. If this was her desire, he would let her know how much she pleased him, and return that pleasure tenfold.

With his mind, he reached out, focusing on the tender spot between her legs, and licked there like a flame dancing over her flesh. He felt her jerk in surprise, breaking the rhythm for a second. A whimper of pleasure escaped her lips as he curled the mental touch deeper, finding the silky, wet nub that pulsed with desire and rubbed against it.

She shuddered, her voice rasping, "How are you doing that?"

"I am a jinn," he said huskily. "In your dreams, I can make anything happen," he stated, and showed her by sliding his energy first inside the tight cavern of her body where she was clenching and hot. The way she moved, rocking back against him as she continued to suck told him he'd guessed right, and he explored further, going deeper, faster, touching parts of her that he was sure had never been known by any other man.

"Oh, Alec," she moaned against him, sighs and moans, the way her body moved in tandem with his magic touch telling him that she was coming. He was, as well, letting himself be more man than jinn in that instant.

He slid deep into her throat, the contractions of her sighs and moans pulling the orgasm from him as he exploded into her. After dazzling moments as she touched and caressed him, he pulled away gently, still hard. She watched in amazement as he hooked both of his arms under hers and lifted her. With one swift movement, her legs wrapping around him instinctively, he planted himself between her legs as deeply as he could go, feeling her stretch to accommodate him.

"I—I already came," she gasped, arching into him even as she objected.

"And you will again, and so will I," he promised, his eyes feasting on her as she held him, her skin rosy, her expression the most perfect image of arousal he'd ever seen.

"This night has only started," he said, drawing back and then thrusting, and again, until they both were lost.

5

NINA WOKE UP SUDDENLY, one eye catching the time on the clock as panic set in. She was two hours late for work. She started to rush from bed, but found her legs wrapped in a tangle of sheets and that she was completely naked. She distinctly remembered going to bed in her underwear. The room looked like a hurricane had hit it, pillows and coverings thrown everywhere. Items on her dresser knocked over, a picture hanging crookedly on the wall.

"What the…?"

She kicked to untangle herself, freezing when a male groan of objection rose in response to her foot hitting something solid. Something solid and…big.

She frantically searched her memory. She hadn't brought anyone home. She'd had a few glasses of wine, alone, brooding over Peter. Then she'd gone to bed—very much alone—and dreamed of…

"Alec," she whispered.

"Yes, sweet?"

What she felt five minutes ago wasn't panic. What she experienced upon hearing the male voice respond to her, *that* was panic.

Disbelief warred with what she was hearing, and she

sent her foot to investigate one more time. It was *his* voice, his strong calf against her instep. She didn't dare move, still trying to figure out if she was sleeping or had drunk more than she thought. Could she have gone out and brought a stranger home, and not even remember it?

When he rolled over, tucking in behind her, a very familiar hard, warm male member nudging at her backside, she yelped and jumped from the bed. Too late, she realized that she hadn't quite freed her legs of the sheets, and she almost fell, but...didn't. Instead, she seemed to stop halfway to the floor, hover, and then was set gently, safely upright again.

Definitely dreaming.

She turned, standing there completely naked, staring into the dark eyes of a real man. A very naked, incredibly hot, aroused man, who was lying in her bed. And he just happened to look exactly like the jinn in her dream. Alec.

"I'm still sleeping. This is one of those weird dreams where you think you've woken up, but you really haven't, right?" she asked as he watched her placidly.

In spite of her hopes otherwise, she knew that she was awake. She heard the car next door pull out of the driveway, the mailman walking down the length of pavement after lifting the squeaking lid on her mailbox to deposit the mail.

Somehow, the man who had done impossible things to her, things no man could do, had ever done, was lying before her, apparently ready and willing to do them again.

"You're real."

"As real as you," he responded matter of factly. "I meant to disappear before you woke up, but—" he broke into a wicked grin that lit his eyes with memories "—you exhausted me."

"*I* exhausted *you?*" she asked incredulously, remembering the hours of erotic play they'd enjoyed. Even if it had only been a dream, she would have still been worn-out. But to think it was real?

Taking a quick mental inventory, she felt refreshed, awake and not even a bit, well, sore. Nina enjoyed sex, but never considered herself a dynamo. The things she'd done last night…and let him do…. She gasped, her hand quickly clasping over her lips in dismay.

"Oh, my God, we didn't even, I didn't have…you didn't use…*protection,*" she almost wailed, trying to remember if she'd taken her birth-control pill the morning before. It had been a little hit-and-miss since Peter, since she wasn't sleeping with anyone else.

Scrambling to the dresser, she reached for her pill pack, but before she could check, his large, bronze hand covered hers. Nina froze in place, looking up into the mirror where he stood behind her, her pale skin against his darker tones, his big, muscular and very naked body making her seem small. She'd never felt small in terms of stature, but Alec… The way his eyes met hers in the mirror had a sliver of heat shimmying all through her nervous system.

"You don't have to worry about those mundane things, Nina. Not with me. I am human, in form and in every way a regular man is, but I am more than that, as you know. You do not risk illness or a child with me…unless the latter is something you want," he said thickly, leaning down to bury his face in the nape of her neck.

She scoffed. "Sure, like my mom used to say, a lot of

babies have been born on someone saying, 'Trust me,'" she said, her breath catching as he nestled closer to her.

"But your mother, a wise woman, no doubt, did not know about jinn. I am a magical creature, Nina. My form is changeable. I am real, but not really," he said somewhat poetically, his breath hot in her ear as she watched him—literally watched him change his appearance before her eyes.

Suddenly, he was light-skinned, blond and blue-eyed. Still big and muscular, but she shook her head in reflex. "Okay, you've proved your point, but I like you the other way," she said truthfully. His exotic dark looks were so different from any other man she'd been with. Maybe that was the attraction.

He rubbed his hands over her shoulders, seducing her into relaxing, and her head rocked back against his chest as she leaned against him. Even though her mind couldn't grasp, entirely, what was happening, her body understood just fine. She was slick and ready when his cock nudged her opening, seeking entrance.

It took the discipline of a thousand women to move away from that tempting nudge, but she put space between them, her sex aching for what he was promising. Her brain was telling her she had to get out, to get away.

"I have to go to work. I can't just stay here all day doing...that," she said, her eyes focused on his erection.

When she looked up, he was smiling again, temptation in his eyes. She took a deep breath, fighting the urge to give in. He was so gorgeous...so perfect.

That thought grounded her. No man was perfect, no person was perfect. This was all some weird, surreal make-believe. In reality, she had rent to pay, and she had to get to work.

"I have to shower and be in the office."

"Let me join you," he said seductively.

She spun around, shouting, "No!" though she didn't really mean to yell, and she took a calming breath. "No. Listen, I don't really understand how this all is possible. Obviously, it's happening but I also have a life and a job, bills to pay. I can't ignore that."

"All you have to do is make a wish, and all of those menial problems would disappear," he said in a very common-sense tone.

She paused, thinking about it. Could life really be that easy? Wish away your problems?

If only. Anyway, she already knew that genie wishes came with a price, and any wish she made might not turn out as she hoped. Look at what had happened with Peter. Her life, messed up as it was, was her own doing, the result of her own choices, and she wasn't about to have it get worse.

"No, thanks. Now, I don't know how this all works, but I really don't want wishes, so, um, you can go back to wherever it is you…live. Here," she said, sliding the ring off her finger. She'd completely forgotten she'd put it back on last night in her wine-influenced mourning about Peter.

"I'm afraid it doesn't work like that Nina. I'm attached to the ring, and whoever has the ring controls my fate. If you make your next two wishes, I will return there until someone else summons me, but that is the only way I would be free. Unless you gave the ring to someone else, and then you give me with it. That is also your choice," he said in a muted tone.

Nina was very uncomfortable with the picture he was painting, that she was stuck with him, unless, like he was an unwanted chair or an old book, she decided to give him away to someone else. And who would she give him to? That definitely didn't feel right. Though he might not be completely human, he was human enough that she couldn't treat him like a trading card.

Blowing out a breath that stirred her bangs, she nodded. "Fine. I wish for a bagel with cream cheese and some coffee. There, that was two, now you're free."

Alec smirked. "I can go get you those things from your kitchen while you shower. I've actually become quite handy with the amenities of modern life, but your wish has to come from your heart. It has to be real."

"I *really* want that bagel," she said, knowing from the look on his face that it was no use.

"I'll get it for you," he said with a small smile. "You shower."

With that, he just blinked out of sight, and Nina was left standing alone in the room, though she could hear him moving around in the kitchen. Unable to comprehend the situation, she gave up and went to shower, then put on one of her old business suits. Armor against the unknown, and against a boss who was probably going to be completely pissed off.

A professional appearance probably wouldn't save her job, but she could hope. She followed the enticing scent of an onion bagel and freshly brewed coffee. Alec was having a cup at her small kitchen table, dressed in worn jeans and an orange T-shirt that made her stop and take him in. He really was magnificent, in and out of his clothes, but the homey look made him seem so real, so normal, that her heart lurched.

"I hope you don't mind I whipped up some of my own

coffee from home, a fresh Turkish blend that's stronger than what you have here, but I think you'll like it. I also took the liberty of getting some pastries."

"You just zapped them in?" she said, sitting down at the table as he poured her coffee and put a bagel in front of her, with a glass of orange juice, the tray of pastries between them.

"No, I just went to the Greek bakery you have down the street—lovely place. Very old-school," he said.

She laughed, and shook her head. "Okay, well, uh, thanks. This all looks wonderful, though I have to get to work or I'm going to be so, so fired."

"Eat. Don't worry. I took care of it."

Nina's hand froze midway to the pastry. "What do you mean?"

"I called your boss."

Alarm reasserted itself so quickly she stood and nearly upset her coffee. "You did *what?*"

"I called your office. The number was on the pad by the phone, and I think you need a proper breakfast after last night," he said casually, his eyes traveling over her suit, approving. "That suit is severe, but it forms to your curves nicely. I'll look forward to taking it off later."

Her cheeks heated, her heart pounding as she thought about him doing just that, and she tried to focus. "What did you do? Did you tell Lindsay I would be there soon?"

Alec grinned. "I did better than that, dear Nina. I told her you were already there."

"Excuse me?"

He waved his hand carelessly, and reached for another pastry. "A little genie confusion...when she sees you, she'll think you were there all morning. You don't have to worry. Sit. Eat."

Nina did sit, mostly because her knees were feeling squishy again. Maybe she did need food.

"So you can do that? Just mess with people's minds?"

He shrugged. "Jinn have different talents, but generally, yes, most can interrupt the pattern of human perception, make them think things are there that are not, or vice versa. It's a parlor trick, mostly, generally meant to protect us against those who would remember too much or share too much about their interactions with us, but some jinn use it for fun, I'll admit. Tricking people into tripping on a sidewalk, or sometimes worse," he said with a hint of darkness in his expression.

"It sounds dangerous."

"A jinn can be dangerous, like any magical creature. As humans do, we have emotions, thoughts, needs, desires, and when crossed, a jinn can cause considerable damage. Or, in the case of Ifrit—"

"What's that?"

"Ifrit are a type of jinn, more generally known for their dangerous natures, their cunning and wickedness. They cannot be all painted with the same brush, of course, but an Ifrit is more…feral…than the average jinn," Alec explained, and then smiled. "Is this for your interview?"

Nina had been listening intently over her breakfast. She realized she was getting information that would make for an amazing story.

"Is there any way to talk to one? An Ifrit?"

Alec seemed to ponder it, and he nodded shortly. "Perhaps. I would have to ask him. There is one more mild-mannered Ifrit I know, who calls himself Joe these days. He's older, and past most of the antics of his youth. He might be willing, or he might want something in exchange. Usually with Joe, it's sex. I could dissuade him from that, unless you would like both of us. That is also possible."

Nina's eyes widened, and the bite of pastry she had almost stuck in her throat. "I, um," she sputtered, coughing. "I don't think so. I'm not that...adventurous."

"Never know until you try," Alec teased, but his eyes remained serious.

"No, but if he would be willing to do an interview, and maybe pose for a photo, it would really get my backside out of a bind."

"And what a lovely backside it is," Alec said again, his gaze warm, making her blush again. She hadn't reacted to a man like this since she was a teenager. *Sheesh.*

"And you?" she said, changing the topic away from her physical attributes.

"Me? You already have me—any way you want me," he said easily. It was her turn to smile.

"No. I meant, will you let me interview you, and maybe get a picture, you know, in your genie getup?"

One dark eyebrow lifted. "My *getup?* If you mean our traditional garb, then yes, though I would change my facial appearance, if you don't mind."

Nina thought about it, and nodded. Often sources wanted to conceal their identities in some way; Alec's method was just a little more extreme than most. "That would be fine."

Finishing her coffee, she stood. "I have to go. You're welcome to hang out here during the day, if you want, unless you have other things to do?"

What *did* he do on his off hours? She marked the question down to ask later.

"Thank you. I will be...around, and I will see you tonight when you return." He promised this with such an intent note of sensuality in his voice that it replayed in her mind as she strolled to the train that would take her to the office.

ALEC WAS TRUE to his word. Up until the moment that she walked through the office—nearly three hours late—she hadn't really believed him. But no one seemed to have any notion that she hadn't been there all morning.

Amazing.

Alec was obviously very real, which made her much more nervous about the article. She wasn't just making something up, playing around with silly facts, and there was no way around that. He could be affected by her report, and more than that, anyone reading it was sure to think she'd really lost her mind. It was darkly ironic that in reporting the truth, in telling what could be the most incredible story of her life, most readers would think it was a lie.

Even more amazing was that it was happening to her and that it was *real*. There was real magic in the world, and suddenly her current job seemed a lot more important and interesting, regardless of what people thought. Either way, reality was shifting on its axis lately.

She knocked on Lindsay's door, then proceeded into her office. "Lindsay, you got a minute?"

"Not quite, but have a seat," her boss said gruffly, not even looking up.

"I have some good news—great news, actually. I have

a genie. I can get the interview, and pictures, probably by day after tomorrow."

That got her boss's attention.

"Are you kidding? You really found the guy? The one they were blogging about?"

"Yep," Nina said, feeling excited about this news, but also apprehensive about protecting Alec. Given her past with protecting her sources, she wanted to make sure she made a good job of the article *and* of making sure Alec was safe. Then again, he was an ancient jinn. It seemed silly to think he needed her protection at all. "He's agreed to answer questions and perhaps even include a friend, a different type of jinn."

The absolute gleam in Lindsay's eye told Nina that she had hit the jackpot jobwise, and relief flooded her. She wouldn't be fired, not today. And maybe she'd get that cover. Cover stories came with sizable bonuses, and writers who spiked weekly sales were often less likely to find themselves investigating pig farms. Having a jinn on the cover would go a long way in making her life more pleasant around here.

"How do you know he's for real?"

Nina felt her cheeks warm. "Well, it's kind of hard to explain, but I found a ring…the same ring that one of the women on the blog found when she met him. Apparently that's how it works. Whoever has the ring controls him, or rather, that's who gets their wishes granted."

"Do you have it?"

"No, I left it in my dresser drawer. I guess it only matters that I own it. I can't quite bring myself to wear it, not after that first time."

"Did you make a wish?" Lindsay was watching her so

closely, Nina had to fight the urge to squirm in her chair. She didn't want to reveal what a disaster her first wish was.

"I did. And he did grant it, though while he granted the literal meaning of the wish, he said he couldn't make other people feel things they didn't feel in the first place. There are some other, uh, limitations on wishing. He's an ancient, magical creature," she said with complete seriousness, which had her pausing to deal with the reality of it all, "and yet he's as human as you and me," she explained, remembering just how human Alec's warm flesh felt pressed up against her own. She didn't intend on sharing *that.*

"This is astounding," Lindsay said on a breath, her tone excited as she stood and then began pacing behind her chair. She stopped, sending Nina a shrewd glance. "I have to admit, I didn't think you'd really do it, but you did. I guess I shouldn't have thought less of a first-rate investigative reporter, huh? When will the article be in to copy?"

Nina hated to admit it, but the praise warmed her. For the first time in a long time, she felt like she was back in form, and straightened in her chair. It was the first time doing work at *The Scoop* felt exciting and important.

"Two more days, tops. But, I want to do this solo—no photographers. I'll get all the shots and do the editing. I want to make sure this is just right," Nina said, holding her breath at making the demands, but Lindsay just nodded.

"Of course, no problem. Tell me, what does this guy look like?"

Nina shrugged. "Well, technically speaking, he can look like anyone. He can be male, female, any race...but to me, I think he looks like..." She paused, crossing her arms over her chest as her nipples budded just thinking about how

Alec looked. Like *heaven* was what she wanted to say, but she kept to the facts. "To me, he looks like a genie, I guess. Darker coloring, black hair, handsome in that exotic way," she continued. "Sometimes he wore his traditional clothes, you know, flowing robes, satin pants and vests, and other times regular clothes, like you or me."

And sometimes, absolutely nothing at all, she added silently. Somewhere in the back of her mind, she thought she heard Alec's sexy chuckle.

"So, get on it. I'm reassigning your other stories this week, and I want you focusing only on this."

Nina smiled. "You got it."

The idea of focusing only on Alec was not a hardship whatsoever, and her job had suddenly become much more appealing.

ALEC FROWNED WHEN HE didn't see Joe at the bar. He didn't know if his old friend would go for being interviewed for a newspaper, but then again, Joe had a huge ego and a sense of adventure.

He spotted the waitress that Joe had been seeing sitting at a table, working on putting menus together. As Alec made his way across the tavern, he saw her pause, set the menu down to wipe the back of her hand across her eyes and grab a tissue.

When he got closer, it was clear she was crying, though she was trying not to.

"Uh, hi," he said uncertainly, trying not to startle her.

She looked at him suspiciously, and then her expression softened. "Oh, hi—didn't I see you talking to Joe the other day?"

"Yeah. My name's Alec."

The pretty woman's eyes flooded with a new wave of tears. "So, he sent his friend to do his dirty work for him?"

Alec was momentarily taken aback. "What? No. I was just wondering if you had seen him. I thought he was usually working the bar in the afternoon."

"He's missed two shifts. He doesn't call, he doesn't answer my messages," she said sadly. "He's already lost the job. They brought in a new guy. No one seems to know where he is," she said, painfully close to a wail.

"He didn't tell you that he was going away?"

"No. That's what I mean. We were supposed to meet at a club after my shift, and he never showed up. His stuff is still at my apartment, except for that stupid lamp he was so attached to, but there's no sign of him. I don't know whether to be frightened for him or pissed off," she said honestly, picking up another tissue. "I don't even know enough about him to call the police and file a report."

"Did you tell anyone?" Alec did not have a good feeling about this. When a jinn just "disappeared" it was usually a bad sign. "And you're sure the lamp was gone?"

"No, what would I tell anyone? I didn't even know his last name. How could I not know that? It's like I never even realized it until I tried to ask around about him, and then I felt like a complete slut, sleeping with a guy and never even knowing his name," she said miserably.

"Did you tell anyone else about you and Joe?"

"I told my friends how great he is…and how it was so romantic when we met when I bought that antique glass lamp at the thrift shop. I picked it up, and he reached for it, too, but let me keep it. It's so weird he would have taken it with him. He's always saying he wants to make all of my wishes come true…and he did, until now."

Alec knelt down, looking around to make sure no one was watching as he took the waitress's hand. She was a delicate little thing, but talked way too much. It would put her in danger as much as it had Joe.

"You don't know anything about Joe because that's how he wanted it, and that's not your fault. You are not a slut, you are a lovely young woman, and everything will be fine. I'll find Joe. You won't worry, you won't be sad, and if anyone else asks, you just tell them everything is fine, okay?"

The girl fell into Alec's sphere of influence very easily, her face clearing of tears, and a smile soon formed. "Yes. I know Joe is just busy or had to pop out of town for a day or so. No problem," she said happily, returning to her work.

Alec nodded. Something bad was going on, and he had to find out what, but he couldn't have this young woman telling everyone about Joe, or drawing attention to the matter.

It didn't take much to figure out that someone had managed to find out his secret and had stolen the lamp. That didn't bode well for Joe's fate.

6

NINA SAT WITH HER LAPTOP balanced on crossed legs, a pen stuck behind her ear as she furiously drafted the leads for her story and sifted through the research, preparing for her interview with Alec.

Unfortunately, he was gone when she'd returned home. Much to her disappointment. She was fired up to start the interview as soon as possible, but with no genie there was no interview.

There was still a part of her that doubted he was real. Maybe the stress and disappointment had become too much, and she had finally just cracked.

She eyed her bed. The past few times, he'd always appeared when she was sleeping—if it weren't for him being with her this morning, she would have continued thinking he was merely a dream.

So this was the test, right? To see if he showed up again, while she was fully awake and waiting for him. Besides, if he found her in bed, they wouldn't end up doing the interview…they'd no doubt find other, more energetic things to do.

The idea had appeal, she thought with a mischievous smile.

"You're sexy when you smile like that." Alec's voice startled her, making her jump, her laptop and everything around her starting to drop. She tried to catch it, but needn't have worried. Alec took everything and set it down neatly and safely on the coffee table.

Well, that settled that as far as the reality test went, she thought, smoothing a hand over her hair.

"You need a bell around your neck or something," she said, jesting, and while he smiled, she saw it didn't reach his eyes. He looked strained, and even tired. Could genies get tired? Another question for her list.

"Sorry. I didn't mean to startle you," he said sincerely, coming over to sit on the sofa near her, the spicy, masculine scent of his skin surrounding her.

"Thanks for saving my laptop," she said, regaining her composure.

He looked at the open screen, and nodded. "Working on your story about me?"

She leaned in, turning the screen away. "Yes. Sorry, but I don't let anyone see my writing before it's as perfect as I can get it. But I would be happy to let you read through it and okay any quotes and information when it's done. Actually, I insist. I want to make sure you are comfortable with whatever I print there."

He stared at her in surprise. "That doesn't seem like very cutthroat journalism."

"Journalists try to beat each other to the punch, and we can be pretty cutthroat to get a story, but if there's one thing I've learned, it's make sure your information is right and take care of your sources," she said, unable to stop a pinch of regret from past failures.

"You didn't fail, Nina. You know that. Someone else did, letting the information about your informant slip into the article you wrote." His tone was soft as he raised a hand and let his fingers thread through her hair. He gently wrapped a few curls around his fingers.

"How do you know about that?"

"I've been in your dreams...I know your secrets. I know what you are capable of and what kind of person you are. I know your heart. You would never have done that, either by mistake or on purpose."

Hearing someone say that out loud freed something inside her, and she felt her eyes sting with tears, and tried to blink them back.

"Thank you, for saying it."

"I mean it. We could try to find out who did it, and why, if you like... All it would take is a wish," he said, his gaze not leaving hers.

She paused, was tempted. How many times had she wondered who had changed the information in that article, who had followed her, found out the source, and printed it, letting her take the fall?

"I would love that," she said carefully, making sure it wasn't expressed as a wish. Alec grinned.

"You're learning...being careful with your words."

"I suppose as much as it would be good to know—to have justice, my name cleared, maybe even to have some kind of revenge...it wouldn't change what happened, would it? Unless I could wish that the entire situation never happened? Can you do that?"

Alec's expression became very serious. "Yes. Though it's very dangerous. Much like I changed your office's perception of your late arrival to work, I could try to change that event, but there is so much more risk…a large change like completely revising something that happened in history. Who knows what the consequences could be? At the very least, you would not have met me."

"Really?"

"Well, if your unfortunate scandal had not happened, and if you had never come to work for the tabloid, you may never have been in that alley looking for genies, now would you?"

She nodded slowly. "No. And I would still be with Peter, not knowing his true nature, that he didn't really love me. I guess it's better how things are this way."

"Even though you hate your current job?"

She shrugged, fudging a little. "I had grander aspirations in life, it's true. But since I've met you, in just these few days, everything seems different. Even if no one ever believes me, I've found the most important discovery I think I could ever manage as a journalist. The truth. It may just look like more crazy tabloid writing, but I know what I know."

Alec looked down modestly. "I am not that important, but it's good that you're feeling better about your life."

"Thanks," she said, realizing it was more true than she'd acknowledged. Everything had changed upon meeting Alec. "You have been more important to that happening than anyone. So I guess as awful as it was, I wouldn't change what happened. None of it," she decided.

"That's a good choice," he affirmed, seeming relieved.

"Where were you today? Where do you go, when you're not here?" she asked, back in journalist mode, grabbing her laptop to take notes.

"I was searching for a friend, the one I told you about.

Joe. He wasn't where he should have been. I fear some harm has come his way."

"What kind of harm?"

"Some people know we are real, have encountered jinn in various guises or points of their lives and will become addicted to the power of wishing. They will sometimes try to trap us, making us their slaves, bending us to their will."

Nina frowned. "You mentioned that, but it's hard to believe an ordinary human being could have any power over a magical creature like yourself. Couldn't you just blip yourself free?"

Alec sighed. "We have some weaknesses. I don't necessarily want you to print what they are."

She took her hands away from the laptop. "Okay, off the record."

He paused, looking at her closely, and nodded. "We can be trapped in various ways—a spell, being locked inside our vessels or being chained."

"Chained? Can't you just slip out of chains like you do clothes?"

"Steel, especially pure iron, is poison to a jinn. It renders us helpless, like the weakest human, and if we are chained in iron long enough, we will lose our magical abilities and can be easily killed. Iron is often used by jinn hunters to capture and allow them to control us."

"Jinn *hunters?*"

"Unfortunately, there are those who think no jinn should walk the earth. There are those whose sole purpose is to rid the world of our kind."

Nina watched Alec's expression change, becoming dark

and more dark. She reached out to touch him, instinctively offering comfort.

"You think that's what happened to your friend Joe?"

"I hope that isn't the case, but he has disappeared. When a jinn disappears from his own kind—we are all able to sense each other, no matter where we are—then it's almost assured that they have been trapped or killed. That jinn's magical essence, their signature, has been erased. The iron will do that, and so will death."

"Have you known Joe for a long time?"

"Over twelve hundred years now…and I have no idea how old he was when I met him then."

She swallowed hard, trying to get her mind around that. The man she was talking to was over a millennium old. But he wasn't really a man, was he?

"Is there anything I can do to help? To find him?" As soon as she said the words, the idea seemed silly, but the question fell from her lips before she could stop it. She almost took it back, but then saw the emotion in his eyes, his lips parting slightly.

"You have the purest heart I have ever known," he said simply, and the distance between them was closed as his firm mouth moved over hers. For long minutes, no coherent thought passed through her mind. When she did separate herself from him for a moment, she realized her laptop was back on the table, and she was wrapped around him, arms and legs, as close as two people could be, almost.

"I am concerned about Joe, but you are my mistress. My duty is to be here with you, to please you," he said seductively, and she felt the warmth of his voice straight down to her toes.

"It doesn't feel right, making you stay here. You should go look for him," she said, though the last thing she wanted was for him to stop touching her.

"There is nowhere to look. If I cannot sense his presence, he could be anywhere, or nowhere," Alec whispered into her ear. The vibration of his voice traveled over her skin, hardening her nipples, making her wet. She gasped when he bit one tender lobe. "And we are here, and alive," he added, pushing her down into the cushions of the sofa and covering her with his body.

She liked the weight of him. Though he was a big man, he didn't feel heavy to her at all, and she parted her thighs instinctively, welcoming him. She knew she wanted him; why pretend? She was going up in flames and couldn't think of anything but having him, so why fight it?

"Yes," he said against her neck, "open for me, Nina."

With one easy movement he was deep inside, and she didn't need to ask how either one of them had become naked. His cock filled every bit of her, stroking the sensitive skin inside her body as his hands moved over the rest of her, tweaking nipples and caressing her thighs until she bucked underneath him. Spasms of release exploded through her body all the way to her fingertips.

"You're so beautiful, so amazing," he crooned. "I love your hair, like black silk."

Nina nearly purred. What on earth could he ever expect her to wish for besides this? Her eyes widened as she felt them gently lifting up, the sofa cushions beneath them gone and only air remaining. She jerked reflexively, but he held her still.

"Shh. I would not let you fall," he reassured her as the

entire room changed around them. She gasped, gazing around as she stayed horizontal, still connected to Alec in the most intimate way possible, but floating amid a magical scene of crystal waterfalls and pungent flowers. She could actually *smell* them.

"H-how…?" she asked, and then smiled. "Never mind. I guess 'how' is just magic."

He moved inside her again, his own jaw tightening as pleasure built. "*This* is magic…the rest is window dressing," he said, his own voice catching slightly. She was moved to think she could cause that kind of pleasure for him.

Nina gave herself over to the fantasy, letting go and floating through the magical space, Alec lifting her up and bringing her forward until his mouth fastened on to the sensitive flesh of her sex. The combined sensations of the floating, the pounding of the waterfall, the succulent scent of the flowers took her out of time, out of place.

She became a creature of pure pleasure, no longer just plain Nina, but something special as Alec's tongue danced over her clit, suckling at the opening to her body, worshipping her with his mouth as they circled and floated. When she came, it wasn't like the normal, earthly orgasms she was used to, but an effervescent kind of pleasure that went on and on, singing through every nerve ending, taking her out of herself to a kind of reality she never imagined was possible.

Nina knew magic was real. She could feel it with every ounce of her soul, and it was Alec who had brought that to her. He'd single-handedly lit up her no-nonsense, career-oriented, boring life with light and imagination.

Her heart squeezed with emotion as her body closed around him again. She brought herself up through the air, smiling at him as she held tight to his broad shoulders and moved. Loving him, giving back, seeing what it took to push her jinn past the limits of his seemingly boundless control.

"Why don't you let me create a little magic for you?" she said as she pushed him back into the middle of the air, the blue pool reflecting beneath them.

"Be careful. You must maintain contact with me to stay suspended," he warned. She smiled back over her shoulder.

"I don't think that will be a problem."

She looked down to find him watching her with hot eyes. In fact, she thought she saw little flames leaping in his irises, but shook off the idea as she stopped teasing and levered herself into a sitting position. Balancing her hands on his thighs, she turned her back to him and took him deep inside her. She heard his hiss of pleasure. She had to admit, the new angle surprised her with its intensity, as well, allowing him to touch her inside in a new way, and snuggling her clit against the base of his cock just perfectly.

"Oh, Alec, this is so good," she said, wanting him to know that no man had ever made her feel this way before. Digging her fingers into his thighs, she wrapped her legs around his hips and started moving, grinding and pumping against him. She lifted one hand from his thigh to delicately stroke the sensitive skin under his balls. She was rewarded when he thrust harder, his hands gripping her backside as they moved in a frantic rhythm that drove them both over the edge.

Pleasure coursed through her, Alec's uninhibited response touching her heart as well as her body. They drifted slowly back down to where he lowered her into the glistening pool, washing her gently. She did the same for him, marveling at the water that was so real, and yet couldn't possibly be. Just like Alec, she thought, tucking in against him.

"I know I shouldn't fall for you, but I'm not sure I can help it," she said plainly. There was no point in subterfuge.

He stroked her hair and she felt his chest rise and fall in a deep sigh.

"I am a jinn, Nina. If I could be with anyone, it would be with you. Of all the women I have known, only you have touched my heart, but I cannot belong to anyone, not truly. I am of fire, you are of earth. I am immortal, you are human. It's how it has always been, and will always be."

"If I don't make my wishes, then you have to stay?"

He tipped her face up to his, and she was surprised to find his gaze filled with pain. "Yes, in that way, I could stay with you, but it means I would have to watch you grow old and eventually die, while I remain the same. I would be free only when I lost you forever, which, my love, I'm not sure I could stand. For both our sakes, it is better that we enjoy what we have, and accept what is."

He'd called her his love. Nina's heart broke a little, but she knew he was right. Keeping Alec with her longer than necessary was wrong for both of them. It would draw out the pleasure, but also the pain.

"You're right," she said bravely, lifting up to press a kiss to his lips and pushing down any pain or fear she felt at the idea of this ending soon. "But I need you to know that before you, I don't think I ever really knew about love. I only thought I did. And when you leave, I'm afraid then I'll really know what it means to lose it, as well."

The thought terrified her. She thought losing Peter had been hard. Losing Peter was nothing.

He nodded, pressing a kiss to her forehead in a gesture so sweet her heart broke again. Wasn't it just her luck that the only man who could really make her happy wasn't a man at all?

7

NINA TAPPED HER PENCIL on the side of her notepad. Something was missing.

After she and Alec had come back to reality, she'd dealt with the mess of emotions she felt for him by pouring herself into work. She started asking him questions, and luckily, he was eager to cooperate.

Eager to finish their business together so he could leave her, she thought, her heart twisting. She couldn't blame him. What future did they have? The idea of growing old while he stayed young and buff held no appeal at all.

Still, staring down at her questions, it was hard not to wonder, what if?

Can jinn have children? she'd asked. *Yes,* he'd said, a warm light in his eye. *But only if they want to.*

Did he have children? No. He'd never found anyone he could imagine being a mother to his children until now.

The words *until now* had nearly undone her, but he'd assured her that she wasn't pregnant—human birth control wouldn't prevent magical progeny, but he had made sure their coupling was safe. Nina, for the first time in her life, wasn't sure if she felt relieved for that fact. Though she loved her work, she'd always hoped to have a family, much like the one she'd grown up in. It had never occurred to her that she couldn't have it all.

She could never have that with Alec, she reminded herself abruptly. Also, he informed her, there was a large chance that his children would be jinn, like their father. Their children would be destined to a life of servitude, as was the jinn's fate, so she couldn't blame them for not having much interest in procreation.

Staring at her questions, she'd drafted the article several times, but still couldn't get it to work. She had all the information she needed, but it wasn't clicking.

Her phone rang, and she saw it was Kaelee.

"Hey, Kaelee."

"You busy?"

Nina could tell from Kaelee's tone that her friend was near tears.

"What's wrong?"

"It's stupid. I just went to meet Chuck, that guy I told you about, at the bar, and he dumped me," Kaelee said flatly. "I don't know why it's getting to me, I don't even know him that well, it's not like—"

"Where are you?"

"Outside your house, in my car."

Nina smiled. "Well, come inside, you nut." She got up to go open the door and found Kaelee halfway up the walk, holding a paper bag.

"What's in the bag?"

"Brownies."

"Perfect."

The two women made their way to the living room, and Nina slung her arm around her pal.

"So what did this jerk give as an excuse for dumping you?"

"He said he wanted someone who was more available. That I worked too much," Kaelee said dispiritedly.

"Ass."

"Well, maybe he has a point. I've been happy focusing on work, and playing the field, but I really liked this guy."

"You shouldn't have to rearrange your life for a man, Kae," Nina said comfortingly.

"I know, but— Hey, what is *this?*" Kaelee swerved off topic as she picked up the men's jeans that Alec had left hanging over the back of the chair.

Nina had nearly forgotten, leaving them there, liking to look at them. They were a reminder that he had actually been there with her, that he wasn't just a figment of her imagination.

Still, with Kaelee staring, waiting, she balked, opening her mouth, then closing it again, unable to find a good answer. She didn't want to lie, but—

"Don't you dare tell me you had Peter the Rat over here…" Kaelee's eyes narrowed suspiciously.

"Oh, no, that's over and done with."

Her friend couldn't hide her surprise or her skepticism. "Really? Just like that? Last I knew, you were pining away, and now you're over him completely?" She cast a glance at the jeans. "These must belong to some rebound stud then, I suppose? Nothing to be ashamed of there, hon. Good for him that he could get you over the hump, so to speak."

Nina bit her lip. "Well…yes and no."

"Tell me about it. It will help me get my mind off

Chuck. I want all of the details," she said lustily, plopping down on the sofa and grabbing a brownie from the bag.

"I don't think you'll believe me, Kae."

"You can tell me anything, Nina, no matter how nuts. I'm your best bud. Shoot."

Nina leaped, needing to talk it out, leaving nothing out from the moment she found the ring in the alley, with the exception of some of the more intimate details.

"And so now, here I am, just completely confused. He's the best man I've ever met, I can't imagine anyone being better for me. He makes Peter look like...a flea."

"He was a flea. Lower than a flea."

"I know, but Alec...he's special. But there's no way we can be together. I seem to have a real talent for falling for the wrong guys."

Understandably, Kaelee did look concerned as Nina explained the many reasons why she and Alec couldn't be together.

"Nina, this isn't like you, and I'm worried."

Nina started to object, reading the clear disbelief on her friend's face—who could blame her?—but Kaelee put up her hand in a silencing gesture.

"I'm not judging, I'm concerned. You're obviously in a bad place right now, and he's just taking advantage of you. Did you give him money? Anything else suspicious? I can have a background check done."

Nina smiled at Kaelee's "lawyer voice." She appreciated her friend's protective instincts, and thought it would be funny to see a background check on a genie who'd been around for over a thousand years.

"I know this all sounds nuts, but no one is taking advantage of me, Kaelee, believe me. It's all real, but I can understand why you'd think I was batty. I could hardly believe it myself for a while. But believe me, Alec is very, very real."

"Ah, Nina, I just don't know what to say to this," Kaelee said, taking a big bite of her brownie.

"I know, it was hard for me to believe, too—that jinn aren't just a fairy tale. Love isn't a fairy tale, either. It's magic, but it's also something you have to protect and cherish, and that takes work, and sacrifice..." Nina drifted off, her thoughts circling.

"I don't think I can write this. It puts Alec, and all jinn, at too much risk."

"Nina, you have to hand in your story—you said this is a cover—that's important!"

"Not as important as protecting what I know now. Protecting Alec and those like him. There's too much at stake here."

"Nina, you have to think more clearly. You're scaring me. Obviously meeting Peter really hurt you, and—"

Nina smiled as she saw Alec appear behind Kaelee. "Kaelee, you need to meet someone."

Kaelee stared at Nina, and then whipped around, jumping up from her seat. She stared at Alec, then Nina.

"You said you were alone here."

"I was. He does that...just blips in," Nina said, watching Kaelee closely. "Alec, this is Kaelee. I hope you don't mind that I told her about you."

"Not at all." Alec smiled at Nina in a way that made her heart tumble.

She had two wishes left, and she could only think of one thing she even wanted to wish for: Alec. But he assured her it didn't work that way. No human could wish a jinn to be other than he is.

"After all, it's coming out in the article, anyway," he said.

"About that...after what has happened to your friend, and what could happen to you, I've decided not to write the article. I'll just work something else out with Lindsay. She won't be happy, but I can make it up to her somehow. I hope."

Alec walked up close, cupping his large hand around her cheek, and Nina forgot they were alone until Kaelee cleared her throat.

"Okay, *Alec,*" Kaelee interrupted in a cool voice, setting her hands on her hips.

Nina smiled. It was her warrior pose.

"Just how many women have you pulled this genie scam on? What do you get? Money? Sex?" Kaelee rolled her eyes, and Nina blushed when she said, "Well, that much is obvious. How can you take advantage of women this way? There are laws, you know."

"I am not a fraud, Kaelee. I would never hurt Nina, and I am a jinn."

Kaelee's lips thinned, which told Nina her friend was getting really pissed.

"Can you show her?" Nina asked. It was important to her that Kaelee understand.

"Nina, please—" Kaelee started to object, and shut up the minute she was lifted from the floor and floating in space.

"Hey! Put me down! How are you doing this?"

Then, Kaelee's clothes changed, and she was dressed first like some exotic princess, and then like a simple farm maiden.

"These are some of your fantasies, yes?" Alec asked,

and Kaelee went pale in midair. It made Nina panic slightly at first, but then she just grinned at Kaelee.

"See?"

Kaelee couldn't answer, her eyes wide and her mouth open in wordless shock as she demanded to be put down, still looking down at her clothes.

"Where are my clothes? What did you put in my drink?" she asked Nina.

"You didn't have anything to drink, hon. Unless there is something a little extra in those brownies, you're as sober as you were when you walked in the door."

"Oh. Oh, my," Kaelee said, sitting again, and looking down to find her regular clothes restored. "How did you do that?"

"It's magic," Alec said with a wicked grin, and changed his clothes, his appearance, and finally returned to standing at Nina's side.

"This is just a little difficult to get comfortable with."

"I understand. For some, it's difficult to realize that our kind are real. That magic is real."

"I guess so. Don't you worry about people knowing?" Kaelee asked.

"I could make you forget," he said casually, "but I think Nina needs you to know that she wasn't making me up. Besides, many, many people in the world know of us, believe in our presence. It has been so since the beginning."

"And I needed you to know I wasn't crazy, and he wasn't trying to take advantage of me," Nina added.

"Oh, there are ways I love taking advantage of you, sweet," Alec said with a wicked smile, and Nina felt her cheeks warm as Kaelee looked on in amazement.

"You lucky duck," Kaelee said with a sudden, matching grin. "If he can do that any time, then you could have—"

"Uh, let's not go there right now," Nina said, interrupting the direction of Kaelee's comments with a laugh.

"Yeah, well, we definitely have some talking to do later," Kaelee promised. Nina was glad that if nothing else, finding out about Alec had certainly distracted her from her gloom about being dumped. Any guy who dumped Kaelee was a loser, as far as Nina was concerned, and her friend deserved better.

"I have to talk to Lindsay, and I'd better do it in person." Nina sighed. "Better to get it over with. She's going to be pissed."

"I think you're doing the right thing, though," Kaelee said. "I can see how people would want to find a jinn, and use them for their own purposes. Wars could be started, for crying out loud."

Alec's eyes darkened, clouded over. "We have been employed in such tragedies, it's true. Our history is a history of slavery, our will and power often bent to the uses of the human thirst for power. Unfortunately, our will is never truly our own."

"That's just not right," Kaelee protested. "All men and women have the right to—"

"I'm not a man, Kaelee. Not really. I am a spirit of fire."

Kaelee stopped cold. "Oh, right. You sure look like a man," she said appreciatively, and Nina rolled her eyes.

"So, I have to go," she said, sharing a long look with Alec. She didn't want to leave him. "You'll be here when I get back?"

He nodded, his gaze fixed on her in a way that made her warm from tip to toe, and Nina heard Kaelee call her a "lucky duck" again under her breath. Nina wasn't sure if she was lucky or not. The whole "better to have loved and lost" bit was wearing a bit thin, to her mind.

"I'll probably have to use my next wish to find a better job," she said gustily, chasing away her morose thoughts. She had to get ready to face Lindsay, and the prospect of being only one wish away from never seeing Alec again.

LINDSAY'S STARE WAS stone-cold, but Nina held it. She knew she was doing the right thing.

"I'm sorry, Lindsay, but I can't do it. You know what happened to me in my old job, that my source was exposed, and it ruined his life. How can I risk that again? Whether anyone believes it or not, some people will know it's real, and it puts these...creatures...at too much risk. I can't live with that on my conscience."

"Listen, Nina, I think you have thrown yourself a little too far into your work. I mean, I go along with a lot of make-believe, too, because if we believe it, we can write it, but you don't expect me to really believe you met a real genie? I mean, I thought you had just found some joker who was pulling one over on these vulnerable women?"

Nina quirked an eyebrow. "And who has made their wishes—their actual wishes—come true? He's real, Lindsay, and I'm not going to sell him out. I just can't. The jinn...too much of their history is defined by slavery and abuse of their power. I don't want to add to that."

Lindsay leaned in over her desk, staring hard. "You expect me to believe you have really found some magical being who grants wishes, and who can grant wishes, change his appearance to whatever he wants, who is poisoned by iron? What game are you playing? Do you have an offer on the story from someone else?"

Nina shook her head and sighed. "No. It's nothing like that."

"So, if jinn are real, Nina, why are you still here? Why aren't you back in your old job, with your former lover? Isn't that what you really wanted anyway?"

"Yes, actually. It was all I wanted, and he made it come true, that Peter wanted to be with me again. However, now I saw the truth about Peter. That he never really wanted me for more than sex. And I saw the truth about this work, too. Lindsay, you know I thought everything we write is crap. I hated it. Then I found Alec, and I realized that there are magical, unexplainable things in the world. And besides, I've also been using Mabel's mud, and it really does work," she said with a small grin. "I guess I found that my past wasn't as great as I thought, and my present wasn't as horrible as I imagined."

Lindsay snorted. "Right, fine," she said, throwing up her hands. "So if that's the case, why not print this story?"

"Because I have a duty to protect them. I can't let this story put Alec or others like him in danger. There are hunters, people who would track jinn down and use them for their own purposes. I can't risk giving out information that would benefit those people, or worse, create more of them."

Lindsay sat down in her chair. "Okay. Fine. You're one of my best reporters, and I don't really want to fire you, so consider this your one big freebie, but if you ever pull this again, you *will* be fired."

Nina blinked. "You mean I'm not?"

"No, but you're going to be pulling some pretty crap assignments for the next few weeks."

Nina grinned, even though she was sure Lindsay probably meant *crap* almost literally, such as was the case with the pig farm. Still, she was ridiculously pleased not to have been fired. If nothing else, she still had two wishes, and a little more time with Alec.

"Can I ask one question?" Lindsay said as she turned to the door.

"What's that?"

"Is this guy living with you? Something a little more personal than the average genie-reporter relationship going on here?"

Nina knew her face had turned red. "He's been staying at my home, but I don't know where he goes when he's not with me. I never even thought to ask. I suppose he's always around somewhere."

"Well, enjoy it while you can, kiddo. And I expect to see you here bright and early on Monday."

"Absolutely."

Nina walked out of the office, closing the door quietly behind her and fighting the urge to rest back on it, her knees shaking.

But there was cause to celebrate. She had Alec in her life right now. She had won an argument based on her strongest principles, and she kept her job.

Smiling, she hurried from the office, planning the evening ahead. So far, Alec had been serving her every need, showering her with magic and offering her anything any woman could want. She was going to serve him for a change, making a perfect dinner, setting the stage for a seduction that he would never forget for another millennium. If she was going to have to lose him sooner or later, she was going to make sure he never forgot their time together.

She ticked off a list in her mind, what she needed to buy, how much time she'd need to make a special meal, pick up a good bottle of wine and treat herself to the expensive lingerie set she'd seen in the window of a local shop. When she'd seen it, she was still mourning Peter, and couldn't imagine wearing the sexy set for anyone else.

Now, she couldn't wait to see Alec's face when he found her in it—and when he took it off.

8

DINNER WAS DONE and simmering, the expensive cut of lamb keeping warm in the oven, but Nina wasn't sure how long it could sit there and not be ruined.

She felt foolish, sitting at the smartly set dining-room table, a half-spent candle softly illuminating an untouched bottle of wine. Sheer scarlet chiffon draped over her limbs, completely transparent but for the scraps of satin that served to cover her breasts and panty line. She'd bought a pretty faux diamond to wear in her navel piercing, which she hadn't bothered with in months.

Staying barefoot, she'd applied her makeup to resemble an exotic harem girl, ready to serve her master. The fantasies she'd cooked up while setting the stage for her seduction of Alec had teased her for hours…but now it was getting late, and there was no Alec. Her fantasies ran cold and she wrapped her arms around her middle, shivering.

Maybe he was out looking for Joe. Maybe he was trying to get some distance. He had no idea she was doing this for him, so it was ridiculous to take it personally. Although tears threatened when she caught her reflection in the dining-room mirror.

Blowing out the candles that adorned the table and

putting the food in the fridge, she walked to her room, deciding it was just too late. Yanking her jeans off the back of the chair, she sighed, wondering what she'd been thinking. Alec had probably been seduced by real harems, given his long lifespan. Maybe it was lucky he'd been late, saving her embarrassment.

Grabbing her laptop, she crawled up on her bed, alone, and surfed the Net, not feeling like doing anything else. The mindless action eventually lulled her to sleep, which she only realized when she woke up, staring at the clock.

Two o'clock in the morning.

No Alec, not in her dreams, not in her bed.

Something was very wrong.

Heart hammering, she sat up, calling out.

"Alec? Are you there? Alec!" She stood, yelling out into the empty room, "Come to me!" and knowing she must be losing her mind, but fear took over. Alec was bound to her. He'd said so himself. If she summoned him, he would hear.

Unless what had happened to his friend had also happened to Alec.

"No," Nina said to herself, making her way to the dresser. Maybe if she had...

The ring.

She pulled every item out of her dresser drawer frantically, dread a cold knot in her chest.

"It's gone. The ring is gone...."

Someone had taken the ring and, with it, Alec.

Kaelee was the only other one who knew...no. Lindsay. Lindsay knew, and suddenly it all added up. Her boss's insistence that she find the jinn, and her glee when Nina had done just that. Her insistence on meeting him, her easy capitulation when Nina had backed down on the story, and the conversation rang in Nina's memory.

You expect me to believe you have really found some magical being who grants wishes, and who can grant wishes, change his appearance to whatever he wants, who is poisoned by iron?

Nina had never told Lindsay about the iron, and Lindsay knew, from their earlier conversation, about the ring, and where Nina had kept it.

Dashing out to her front door, Nina slid her fingers underneath the ledge of the stone leading up to her apartment, where she taped her spare key. It was there, in the dirt—the tape had been removed.

Only two people knew about that key, Kaelee and Lindsay. Kaelee would never do such a thing. It had to be Lindsay.

"Oh, God," Nina said, feeling sick as she paced. Here she had been wasting time all day, all evening, feeling stupid and sorry for herself. Of course Alec would be here, if he could.

She had been so caught up in her plans and her pity party that she never imagined anything bad could have happened to him. And if anything really bad *had* happened, how could she not be to blame? Why had she not thought of the ring earlier? She'd been gone most of the afternoon shopping. Lindsay had plenty of time to come here, get the ring, and take him…where?

She grabbed her cell phone, and called the only person she could call at 2:00 a.m. about a missing jinn.

"Kaelee?"

"Uh, yeah?" Her friend was groggy, probably awakened from a deep sleep.

"I need you. Someone has taken Alec—I think it might be Lindsay. I think she's the jinn hunter."

"THIS MAY NOT have been such a great idea," Kaelee whispered, holding the flashlight on the door while Nina tried to pick the lock of Lindsay's office. The offices didn't have security cameras; there was just a night guy who walked through now and then. He wasn't too enthusiastic about his job, watching a game where he was sitting in his office, and waving her on when she'd stopped to explain.

Still, Lindsay's office was off-limits and locked.

"When does the security guy come through?"

"I have no idea, but hopefully not before we have what we need. I couldn't find Lindsay's address in the phone book, and nowhere on the directory we have at home. Everyone is on that directory, except for her. I never noticed before."

"Does the security guy have a gun?" Kaelee asked worriedly.

"Nah, probably not," Nina said with far more certainty than she felt.

"*Probably* not?"

Nina had once learned to pick locks while researching a story on urban theft, but she was rusty. "Ah! There we go. We're in," she said with a quiet hoot of victory.

"I'm a lawyer, I could get disbarred for this. I really should have—"

"I'll be as quick as I can, Kaelee. You stay out there, and keep watch. I appreciate this more than I can say. You're the absolute best friend in the world," Nina said sincerely, knowing what she had asked of Kaelee, who always followed the rules.

Kaelee shrugged. "Fine. Who needs a career, right?"

"I'll hurry and see what I can find. This bitch has to live somewhere, and she has Alec."

"I know. That's why I'm here. So go look, already," Kaelee urged, not taking her eyes off the main door.

Nina didn't dare turn on the overhead light, but pulled open drawers, searching for anything personal that would have Lindsay's address. She really didn't want anyone knowing where she lived, and there had to be a reason for that besides privacy.

She saw what looked like the same icon used on her own telephone bill and grabbed at the slip of paper buried within a bunch of other documents. Yanking it out, she hooted with success before becoming very quiet.

"What? Did you find something?" Kaelee said from the doorway.

"Oh, yeah," Nina replied, seething with anger. "Check out this telephone bill."

Kaelee took it and shrugged.

"The address, Kae, look at the address. I don't think there's any way Lindsay makes enough to live there unless she's up to something nasty," Nina said, knowing exactly how her boss must manage to maintain a residence that overlooked the ocean, high on one of the most coveted locations just outside Boston in Marblehead.

"Maybe it's a family home? Old money?"

"Yeah, really old. Like, thousands of years old. She's obviously a jinn hunter. She uses her resources here at the paper to track them down, or in this case, has us do her hunting for her, and then she sells them to people who want to use them or hurt them, thus keeping up this kind of lifestyle."

"Unbelievable skank," Kaelee breathed. "But what do we do? If she's able to control them, how do we stand a chance?"

"She's just a woman, and she doesn't know we're on to her. We have the element of surprise."

"Do we know what to do with it?" Kaelee asked.

Nina hugged her friend. "Hey, you don't have to go any further than this. Alec is mine, uh, I mean…my responsibility. And I'm the one Lindsay used to do her dirty work, to find her way to him, and probably to Joe, too. I can do this alone. But wait for me to come back and if I don't, send the police to that address."

"Do you know exactly what it is you're going to do?" Kaelee asked, crossing her arms over her middle.

Nina pursed her lips. "You mean, do I have a plan?"

"Yeah."

"I figured I'd get one between here and there."

"Probably the easiest thing to do is stake out the house, and wait until she leaves. Then just sneak in and free them. And if you need me, I'm there. I've come this far, what's breaking a few more laws to win back the man you love?"

Kaelee's words stopped Nina's mind cold. "I don't, I mean, I can't… He isn't…"

"Do you love him, no matter what he is or isn't?"

Nina blinked hard to prevent tears. She couldn't afford tears right now. "Yeah, I do."

"Do you think he feels the same?"

"I think so, but there are too many obstacles, and I'm not even sure if I care that we can't be together forever."

Kaelee smiled and reached out to hug Nina. "Hate to break it to you, kiddo, but no one is together *forever.* You just have to take what comes your way, and enjoy it. And by my count, you have two more wishes left. I say draw them out as long as it's still good for both of you."

Nina's hope blossomed as she took in her friend's words. If she could find Alec and get him back, could she convince him to stay with her for as long as they both wanted to be together? Would it make eventual parting worse?

"Well, okay then. But my car will stand out like a sore thumb. I don't think we have the time to stake out the neighborhood. I just have to go in there and try to take back what's mine," Nina said, sounding braver than she felt.

Kaelee tapped a finger on her chin. "Then what we need is a distraction. Something to give you time to get in and out quickly."

"You're right. Okay. This is the plan…."

"MA'AM, I'VE BEEN sent by the city hall to administer a questionnaire about your neighbor's petition to…"

Nina heard Kaelee at the front door of Lindsay's mansion and knew it was now or never. Sneaking around the side of the humongous house, she peeked in one window after another until finally she saw what she was looking for, and held back a gasp, by clasping her hand over her mouth.

She couldn't believe her eyes. Though she didn't see Alec, a Nordic-looking man was shackled to a wall with heavy iron chains. Her heart broke a little as she stared at Alec's friend, bloody lashes covering most of his body. He was naked, and Nina averted her eyes. His dignity had been more than abused, and she wasn't going to add to it by gawking.

Now she had to figure out how to get in. Jiggling at the window, she found it snug.

Cursing, she checked along the entire side of the house and finally found a basement window that gave way as she pushed on it, creating space just wide enough for her to sneak through. She could still hear Kaelee chattering on out front, so she was okay, but she had to move fast.

Pausing for a moment to get her bearings, she tried to figure where the room was that held Alec and his friend. It had looked like a library or a study. Quickly she dashed up a set of stairs, heading left down a long hallway.

Coming around a corner, she heard a noise and froze. *Stupid.* She had assumed Lindsay lived here alone. What if there was someone else in the house?

Swallowing hard, she slipped into a nook and peeked, only to see a gray cat, rubbing the side of his head on the corner as he looked up at her inquisitively.

"Hey, I know you," she said, narrowing her eyes at the cat. "You were the cat in the alley."

The cat purred loudly and turned away, walking down the hall. He stopped, looking at her, and the message in his eyes was clear. *Follow me.*

Nina grimaced, but the way her world had been flipped upside down lately, who was she to argue?

Stepping lightly, she followed the cat down the hall, through a few archways, and then heard the front door slam. Uh-oh. Kaelee's ruse was up and time was running out.

"Hurry, kitty, I need to find them and the ring," she

urged and the cat moved more quickly until Nina found herself standing before a closed door. It had to be the room where she'd seen Alec and his friend. The cat purred around her feet.

"Thanks, kitty, whoever you are," she whispered. Some magical friend of Alec's, she figured as she opened the door. She closed it quietly; she could hear someone humming. Lindsay.

She ran to Alec, shaking him, and he groaned. She heard a growl from the other side of the room, and turned to find the other jinn glaring at her, his eyes wild.

"Shh… Joe? I'm Nina. I'm here to help. I'm a friend of Alec's."

Joe eyed her warily, but stopped growling.

Nina didn't hear the humming anymore and had no idea where Lindsay was. Spotting a chair by the edge of the wall, she wedged it under the door to buy her more time, and set about loosening the chains that bound Alec, who was stripped to his briefs, but appeared unharmed, she realized with relief.

"Alec, c'mon, Alec, I need you conscious," she said.

His eyes fluttered briefly, and he winced, stretching his arms and legs.

"Nina? What are you doing here?" he finally said, groggy but eyeing the chains that had him bound to the wall.

"Has she hurt you?" Nina asked, unlocking his chains, her eyes scanning his gorgeous body.

"No, not yet. She's been, uh, taking her time with Ahja, I mean, Joe," he informed her, anger brimming in his eyes as he looked at his friend.

"I'm here to help you escape."

Alec shook his head sadly. "I can't escape. She has the ring, and I am bound to whoever has it."

"Then I guess I have to get it back. Do you know where it is?"

"Probably on her person, I would guess. She wouldn't let it go far."

Nina sighed. "Well, that's a problem. Can you help me take it from her?"

Alec placed his hands on her shoulders, looking between her and the door with what seemed like great worry.

"Nina, you have to leave. I don't want to hurt you."

Nina drew back. "Why would you hurt me?"

"If she has the ring..."

Awareness dawned. "She could wish for you to hurt me. I get it," she said on a whisper. "The bitch."

"Yes."

"Then we'd better get the jump on her, hadn't we?"

"Nina—" Alec began to object.

"No, Alec. I'm not leaving you, and we're not leaving him." She nodded toward the other jinn. "Who knows how many jinn she's done this to, and it has to stop."

"You have no idea—"

Their argument ceased as they heard footsteps coming down the hallway. Nina moved away from Alec, taking her position by the door and quietly sliding the chair back into place.

"When she comes in, distract her," Nina said softly. "She won't expect you to be free, and that will give us the element of surprise." She put her back to the wall. Reaching next to her in the dimly lit room, she closed her hand over the first object she found on a shelf that filled the space next to her.

The door opened, pushed inward, and Lindsay, dressed from head to toe in dominatrix black leather, walked in, not noticing Alec at first.

"Sorry for the interruption, boys. Now, I'm changed and… You! What are you doing out of your chains?"

She stepped toward Alec, who brought himself up to his full height and glared at her.

"I suppose you thought that—"

Nina cut the thought off short, bringing the heavy object in her hand down hard on Lindsay's head, and hoping it was enough.

Her boss collapsed in front of her, and Nina froze, still holding the heavy antique in her hand as she waited to see if she'd delivered a knockout.

"Score!" she said under her breath as she toed Lindsay. She saw that Lindsay didn't move, but observed the pulse still kicking hard at the base of her throat.

"Now let's see where you hid the ring, boss," Nina said, patting Lindsay down in the leather, and finally finding the ring under the skintight top she wore, hanging by a chain around her neck.

Nina looked up at Alec, who watched quietly, their eyes meeting as Nina slipped the ring on her finger and they became bound again. The relief was palpable, their bond a tangible thing between them as she couldn't resist crossing the room and throwing herself into his waiting arms.

"I was so frightened, Alec. I didn't know if I would ever see you again," she admitted, too relieved to hold back.

"I know. I felt the same, my love," he said, burying his face in her hair.

As they separated, she checked on Lindsay. "I'll chain her, and we can decide what to do next, but we have to help your friend Joe."

Alec looked at Joe, who eyed them darkly, and nodded. "You bind her, but Joe…he's taken too much. She pushed him too hard. If I let him go, he'll hurt you. He'll hurt anyone in his path."

A low growl came from the other side of the room, as if confirming Alec's words.

Nina's heart sank. "You can't kill him. You can't possibly mean that?"

Alec shook his head. "No, but he has to be contained. He has to heal, to come back to himself. That could take tens or hundreds of years," he said sadly.

"How?"

Alec nodded at the heavy glass lamp on the floor where she had dropped it. She'd used it as a weapon, not realizing its importance.

"The lamp is Joe's talisman, much like my ring. Whoever holds it, commands it. If you take it, you can command him. You can tell him to go there. He will have no choice. He won't be free, but he won't be dead or able to hurt anyone else. I can take him where he will be safe."

Nina nodded as she finished securing the chains around Lindsay and then picked up the lamp. It was large and thick, the rose glass so thick that when she held it to the window, it seemed to radiate with a thousand sparks of light.

"His real name is Ahja?"

Alec's expression was gravely serious. "Nina, no one should ever speak a jinn's real name. To know that…it grants too much power. But yes, that is his name. No one can ever know."

"I promise," she said softly, walking up closer to Joe. As close as she dared to get.

"Joe, I command you to your vessel, where you are to stay until you are healed from this terrible ordeal," she said with both authority and remorse.

The man before her struggled against his chains, his mad eyes glaring and fixing on her as if she were the devil incarnate. The chains were left dangling from the wall as he melted into the lamp, where Nina quickly replaced the cover.

"There. He's safe now," she said, handing the lamp to Alec.

"No!" came a scream from the other side of the room, and they realized with a start that their quarry had awakened. Lindsay struggled with her chains, but only tired herself trying to escape them, eventually collapsing to the floor, breathing heavily. Nina could feel the waves of hatred emanating from Lindsay.

"I won't stop—you'll have to kill me. And you can't do that, can you, Miss Goody Two-shoes?" she sneered.

"I can," Alec threatened in a low tone of voice and stepped forward. Lindsay shrank back to the wall, fearful as she should be, Alec looming over her.

Nina took the lamp from Alec and placed it on the desk, staring at it and thinking of Joe. She touched Alec's arm. "No. I have a better idea…"

"Alec, I wish she should live her life as if she had never met a jinn, never knew a jinn and has no knowledge about jinn," Nina said, the full weight of her heart behind the wish. "That she could have no knowledge any of this ever happened." Alec smiled, and Lindsay went pale with absolute terror.

"No, you can't, I won't—"

Alec walked up close to where the woman kneeled on the floor, and then squatted down, staring at her hard. "It is done."

Nina took a deep breath, nodding, and watching as Lindsay blinked, pale and confused, scanning their surroundings.

"Where am I? Nina, why are we here? What's going on?"

"Don't worry, Lindsay. We were working on a story, and you're safe now." Nina looked at Alec. "We all are."

"There are others," he said, glancing at the lamp, then going over to lift it. "I must take this where he will be safe."

She nodded.

"I'll be back," he told her and leaned in, pressing his lips to hers. "You still have a wish left. One," he reminded her.

She smiled. "I know."

Then he was gone, and she turned to face Lindsay.

"You're going to be fine. It's all over now," she said coldly, unable to muster any sympathy. Nina undid her chains and helped her stand. Lindsay lifted a hand to her head.

"How did I get hurt?"

"You don't remember?"

"I don't remember anything about this." Lindsay looked at her, blood emptying from her face as she sagged a little, and Nina caught her, before she slipped to the floor.

"Don't worry about it. You're fine now."

NINA PACED THE LIVING ROOM of her home, tense and wired.

It was over now, twenty-four hours later, and all she wanted was to have Alec back here.

No sooner had she thought it and he was there, a solid male wall of muscle that she walked directly into on her next traverse of the room.

"Oh!" she said, planting her hands on his chest. "You're here."

He smiled down. "Yes. I'm back. With you."

He dipped down, capturing her mouth in a hot kiss, and she was trembling before he let her go. "You came for me. You saved me and Joe. I made sure the powers that be know the story."

"Oh. Who are the powers that be?"

He shrugged with a grin. "They are who they are."

She rolled her eyes, then became serious again. "You took everything she knew about the jinn, didn't you?"

His mouth, which had moved over hers so sensually just moments before, hardened to a flat line.

"I had to. She had been doing this for a long time, researching jinn since she was a young woman, trapping them for over a decade. She'd first learned about them through research her parents had done. Knowledge of them was woven into every level of her existence, and she'd used them…for everything. Even if she comes across the topic again, it won't register or stay with her. Ever."

Nina frowned, saddened by all that had been lost.

"Shh," he said, rubbing his thumb lightly over her lips and raining gentle kisses on her face. "It's done now. It's in the past."

Just being next to him kindled little fires from head to

toe. The darkness that had hovered over her all day seemed to lift as his arms came around her, picking her up and taking her to bed. There his lips finally found hers, plundering like a desperate, hungry man who'd been away from his lover too long.

Or who planned on being away from her for a very long time to come.

Though she was breathless, and it was hard not to be distracted by the hardness that he was pressing into the *V* of her body, she broke the kiss and settled her forehead against his.

"Alec?"

"Yes, my love?" He responded while nibbling on her ear in a most delectable way.

"I know what I want for my third wish."

He stilled beneath her hands, silent, his surprise settling like a chill between them.

"Of course," he said stiffly. "All you need to do is ask."

She smiled, her heart hammering in her chest as she made him look at her, saw the emotions that tore him apart reflected in his eyes. There was pain etched into the regal planes of his handsome face. He really did love her. She leaned in to kiss him.

"My wish is that you should have your heart's desire…that whatever you would wish for, you should have it. I'm giving my last wish to you, Alec, to do with as you please."

Tears filled her eyes as she saw the shock in his expression, her heart full of joy. His fingers trembled slightly as he drifted them tenderly over her cheek, his voice rough.

"This cannot be undone, Nina. To bequeath a wish…it is almost never done."

"I love you, Alec. All I want is for you to be happy, for you to have whatever you wish for."

He set her down, the two of them standing close together, his hands on her shoulders. His expression was so solemn, so intense, that Nina almost worried that he would refuse her. What if she had guessed wrong? What if the wish didn't turn out right? What if he didn't want what—

"Nina, I wish for nothing more than to live a mortal life with the woman I love...with you. You are my heart's desire, and I wish to spend all of my remaining human years with you," he said the words like a vow, and something shimmered slightly between them. A golden haze of sparks wrapped around them both and then disappeared in the blink of an eye.

He looked down at her. "It is done, and cannot be undone. I am only a man now." The uncertainty in his eyes moved her deeply. "I dearly hope that this is what you wanted, my love..."

Pushing up on tiptoe, she pulled him down to kiss him passionately, letting tears flow freely.

Alec was hers. He was real, he was human, and he wanted to be with her.

"You're all I ever wanted, Alec—more than I ever could have wished for," she said against his mouth. Her hands drifted over him, finding him hard, his breathing urgent. His hands covered her breasts, pushing her shirt up, momentarily struggling with the clasp on her bra as they laughed together over this minute clumsiness.

"I've never had to do this without magic before," he admitted a little bashfully, finally releasing her from the bra. She watched him intently as he took great pleasure in removing the rest of her clothes with his hands instead of just blinking them away.

She did the same for him, kissing every inch of exposed flesh as she did so, immensely happy about the incredible responsiveness of his body to her touch.

"I feel...*more.* I never imagined that I could feel more as a man," he said in wonder. "Without magic, I didn't know what to expect, but it's as if everything has come alive. It's all rich and real, and amazingly alive." He spoke with a deep, sexy laugh, catching her up close to him, every inch of their bodies pressed together, as if he couldn't get enough.

She smiled through the kisses, her heart full. They sought each other in the most humanly intimate way possible, falling back to the bed. As their bodies and hearts joined, no more words were necessary as all of their wishes came true.

Harlequin offers a romance for every mood!
See below for a sneak peek
from our paranormal romance line,
Silhouette® Nocturne™.
Enjoy a preview of REUNION by USA TODAY
bestselling author Lindsay McKenna.

Aella closed her eyes and sensed a distinct shift, like movement from the world around her to the unseen world.

She opened her eyes. And had a slight shock at the man standing ten feet away. He wasn't just any man. Her heart leaped and pounded. He reminded her of a fierce warrior from an ancient civilization. Incan? She wasn't sure but she felt his deep power and masculinity.

I'm Aella. Are you the guardian of this sacred site? she asked, hoping her telepathy was strong.

Fox's entire body soared with joy. Fox struggled to put his personal pleasure aside.

Greetings, Aella. I'm the assistant guardian to this sacred area. You may call me Fox. How can I be of service to you, Aella? he asked.

I'm searching for a green sphere. A legend says that the Emperor Pachacuti had seven emerald spheres created for the Emerald Key necklace. He had seven of his priestesses and priests travel the world to hide these spheres from evil forces. It is said that when all seven spheres are found, restrung and worn, that Light will return to the Earth. The fourth sphere is here, at your sacred site. Are you aware of it? Aella held her breath. She loved looking at him, especially his sensual mouth. The desire to kiss him came out of nowhere.

Fox was stunned by the request. *I know of the Emerald Key necklace because I served the emperor at the time it was created. However, I did not realize that one of the spheres is here.*

Aella felt sad. Why? Every time she looked at Fox, her heart felt as if it would tear out of her chest. *May I stay in touch with you as I work with this site?* she asked.

Of course. Fox wanted nothing more than to be here with her. To absorb her ephemeral beauty and hear her speak once more.

Aella's spirit lifted. What *was* this strange connection between them? Her curiosity was strong, but she had more pressing matters. In the next few days, Aella knew her life would change forever. How, she had no idea….

Look for REUNION
by USA TODAY *bestselling author Lindsay McKenna,*
available April 2010, only from
Silhouette® Nocturne™.

HARLEQUIN®
INTRIGUE®
WILL THIS REUNITED FAMILY BE STRONG ENOUGH TO EXPOSE A LURKING KILLER?
FIND OUT IN THIS ALL-NEW THRILLING TRILOGY FROM TOP HARLEQUIN INTRIGUE AUTHOR
B.J. DANIELS
WHITEHORSE MONTANA
Winchester Ranch
GUN-SHY BRIDE—April 2010
HITCHED—May 2010
TWELVE-GAUGE GUARDIAN—June 2010

HARLEQUIN®
Presents®

2 Stories in 1

COMING NEXT MONTH

Available March 30, 2010

#531 JUST FOOLING AROUND
Encounters
Julie Kenner and Kathleen O'Reilly

#532 THE DRIFTER
Smooth Operators
Kate Hoffmann

#533 WHILE SHE WAS SLEEPING...
The Wrong Bed: Again and Again
Isabel Sharpe

#534 THE CAPTIVE
Blaze Historicals
Joanne Rock

#535 UNDER HIS SPELL
Forbidden Fantasies
Kathy Lyons

#536 DELICIOUSLY DANGEROUS
Undercover Lovers
Karen Anders

www.eHarlequin.com

HBCNMBPA0310